"If you don't want me to kiss you, push me away right now."

"You're wasting time." Amy slid her arms around Riley and pulled him close.

His mouth took hers and he invaded her senses, heating her blood, her skin. Stealing her breath. Softening her heart. She drank him in, reveled in him. Never had she felt so complete. And never had a kiss made her yearn so strongly for more.

They might have kissed forever but for the sound of three little girls giggling.

Riley and Amy tore apart, chests heaving, eyes wide. "Wow," he whispered.

She couldn't help but smile. "Yeah." Then she remembered who she was kissing, and her heart sank. It shouldn't have happened, that kiss.

And it damn sure shouldn't have been a *wow*.

Dear Reader,

Like many of you, I grew up on heroes. The first one I remember adoring was Roy Rogers, but there were others. They were anyone in uniform—police officers, firefighters, soldiers, sailors. They were mommies and daddies, big brothers and sisters. Stepdads and stepmoms. And of course, they were cowboys. All of these people are automatically heroes to me, until and unless they prove otherwise.

It was a long time before I realized that my own mother belonged in this category. Not because she saved anyone's life, but she gave me life, nurtured me, raised me, taught me, gave me a strong set of values and, always, always, she loved me, and expected nothing in return. What a hero.

But every now and then someone you wouldn't normally think of as deserving accolades steps up when called and, without thinking, risks it all for someone else. That's a hero, too. Even more so if they're scared and do it anyway.

That's what this TRIBUTE, TEXAS, series has been about—ordinary people doing extraordinary things, and my small way of paying tribute to them.

Happy reading,

Janis Reams Hudson

RILEY AND HIS GIRLS

JANIS REAMS HUDSON

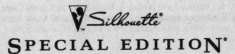

SPECIAL EDITION®

Published by Silhouette Books
America's Publisher of Contemporary Romance

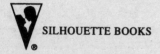 SILHOUETTE BOOKS

ISBN-13: 978-0-373-24796-7
ISBN-10:   0-373-24796-6

RILEY AND HIS GIRLS

Visit Silhouette Books at www.eHarlequin.com

Printed in U.S.A.

JANIS REAMS HUDSON

is the prolific author of more than thirty-five novels, both contemporary and historical romances. Her titles have appeared on the bestseller lists of Waldenbooks, B. Dalton and Bookrak, and have earned numerous awards, including Reviewer's Choice awards from *Romantic Times BOOKreviews* and a National Reader's Choice Award. She's a three-time finalist for the Romance Writers of America's coveted RITA® Award, and is a past president of that 10,000-member organization. As a child of the West, Janis was born in California, grew up in Colorado, lived in south Texas and now calls central Oklahoma home, where she and her husband, Ron, live with their various cats, ducks, sheep and Jack I. B. Squirrel.

Chapter One

Amy Galloway parked her eight-year-old car at the curb on the tree-lined street and got out. Her stomach was dancing in her gut as if a volley of rocket-propelled grenades was being lobbed over her head. The house, a ranch-style in pale-gray brick, was as beautiful and welcoming as she'd known it would be. There was no reason to be nervous.

From inside the house came what sounded like a female wail of distress. Maybe she had come at a bad time. Maybe she should wait—no. She was here, and she had a purpose. She owed Brenda more than she could ever pay.

That wail came from the house again. Someone definitely seemed more than a little upset.

Inside the house, someone *was* more than a little upset.

"Daddy, Cindy keeps untying my ribbon," Jasmine whined at the top of her lungs.

Riley Sinclair gave his jaw one final swipe with the razor, then rinsed off the blade before grabbing his shirt and slipping it on. "Cindy," he called on his way to the hall. "Did you untie Jasmine's ribbon?"

"Yes." For a four-year-old, she sounded amazingly self-assured.

Riley stopped in the doorway to the girls' bedroom. "Why?"

Cindy crossed her arms and tilted her head. Her eyes were narrowed, her expression serious. "Because it was ugly."

"It was not," Pammy yelled. "I tied it myself."

"Mommy would have tied it better," Cindy said. She'd gone from serious to snotty in a blink.

Riley wanted to close his eyes, turn around and go back to bed. Maybe if they started this day over, it would go better. This was the girls' third row in the past half hour.

Since starting over wasn't an option, he wanted to yell, *Stop it!* But he couldn't. Especially not after they'd brought their mother into the fray. He said a quick, oft-repeated prayer for patience.

"Well, Mommy's not here," Pammy shot back, just as snotty.

"Pammy," he warned tersely. "Watch your tone."

"Well, it's true." As the oldest, nine-year-old Pammy, felt their mother's loss the most. "I can't help it if I can't tie a bow like Mommy, or make French toast like her, or anything else." Tears filled her eyes.

Six-year-old Jasmine saw the wet streaks on her big sister's cheeks and started crying.

Cindy, the youngest, followed suit and wailed.

Riley's throat tightened. His vision blurred. He wanted to join them and wail out his misery. He missed Brenda, too. And he knew exactly how Pammy felt. He wasn't as good a cook or house-keeper, or knee-bandager, or hair-comber, or story-teller, or doll-dresser or any of those other things Brenda used to do with the girls before the National Guard activated her and sent her to Iraq.

She hadn't wanted to die any more than he'd

wanted her to get herself killed. But Riley understood that other tone in Pammy's voice, too. It was hard sometimes not to feel anger at losing the glue that had always held your life together. For Pammy, Brenda had been her glue since she'd been born. For Riley, since he'd fallen for Brenda in first grade.

But he didn't have time to remember those good days. Not now. "Come here, babies." He pulled all three of the girls into his arms and held them.

When they finished crying, he dried their tears. Pammy retied Jasmine's hair ribbon into a bow, one that Cindy finally approved of. Peace on earth.

Peace that was interrupted about thirty seconds later when the doorbell rang.

"I'll get it!" Pammy asserted her authority as oldest child.

Jasmine forgot her earlier tears and raced after Pammy. "*I'll* get it!"

"No, let me, it's my turn." His youngest and smallest daughter nearly bowled him over as she shoved him aside on her way to the front door.

"What's the rule?" he called out sharply. They might live in small-town Texas, but that didn't mean they shouldn't exercise basic precautions.

"But, Dad, it's Saturday," Jasmine cried.

He caught up with them in the foyer just as Jasmine put her hand on the doorknob. "What's the rule?"

The doorbell rang again.

"Be right there," he called out. Then, to the girls, "What's the rule?"

"Never open the door unless you know it's a friend."

"That's right. And does it say anything about Saturday?"

Cindy pouted, Jasmine hung her head. Pammy said, "No, sir. I looked. It's a lady. She looks kinda familiar, I think."

"All right." He opened the door. The woman standing there was about five-six and wore a blue plaid flannel shirt, tail out, over faded blue jeans with new sneakers on her feet. Her skin was tanned, with a bridge of freckles across her nose and cheeks. Her hair was pulled back tightly into a knot at the base of her skull. It looked brown, but from his angle it was hard to tell. Her eyes were the green of new leaves. The apprehension he read in them puzzled him. "Hello," he said.

Amy stared at the man before her, at the three little girls vying for position around him in the doorway. This was a picture come to life right before her eyes. Any one of a dozen pictures, in fact, carried by her best friend and fellow sergeant Brenda Sinclair in Iraq and shown off to anyone and everyone who would look. Brenda had been so in love with this man, so adoring of their daughters.

"What can I do for you?" the man asked.

Amy pulled her mind from the past and focused on the here and now. "Mr. Sinclair?" she asked. Stupid to ask. She knew it was him. But she was unaccountably nervous, with an entire platoon marching in step just behind her breastbone. "Riley Sinclair?"

"That's me." He cocked his head and peered at her more closely. "Do I know you?"

"I told you she looked familiar," the oldest daughter said.

"We've never met," Amy told him.

"Daddy?" The smallest girl sidled up next to him and tugged on his arm.

"Just a minute, sweetie."

The little girl looked up at her daddy, then at Amy. Amy smiled. "Hello."

The child snuggled closer to her father and smiled at Amy as she spoke to him. "She looks like Sergeant Amy on the fridge."

Startled, Amy stared at the child.

"By golly, Cindy, she does, doesn't she?" the man said. "You are, aren't you?" he asked her.

Amy frowned. "The fridge? Wha...? I don't...?"

"My wife sent a photo home from Iraq of her and her friend. It's you." He sounded...awed.

Amy had the strongest urge to glance over her shoulder to see who he was talking to.

"Amy?"

Realizing that she'd left him standing there, she suddenly smiled and offered him a hand. "I'm sorry. Yes, I'm Amy Galloway. You're Riley, and these must be your daughters."

The child's eyes widened. "You know who we are?"

"Of course I do. Your mother told me all about you."

"She did?" the smallest one asked.

"In Iraq?" the middle one asked.

"Before she died," the oldest one stated flatly.

"That's right," Amy told them.

"She was a sergeant, too," the oldest said.

"That's right." Amy ached with the need to pull these sweet babies into her arms and hold them, keep them safe, love them.

But they didn't need her, she reminded herself. They had their father for all of that.

"I wonder," she said to him, "if I might have a few minutes of your time, Mr. Sinclair?"

"Of course," he answered easily. "Girls, clear a path and let the sergeant in."

Amy shook her head. "Call me Amy. I'm a civilian now."

"No kidding?" His smile widened. "Is it congratulations or condolences?"

While most people assumed she should be ecstatic to be out of the army, this man understood that she might feel otherwise. She appreciated that. "A little of both," she said honestly.

She followed him past the living room on the right, the formal dining room on the left, and into what Brenda had called the great room. Kitchen at one end, television, sofas, a wingback chair and a pair of recliners, along with bookshelves and a full entertainment center at the other.

Amy breathed a sigh of relief. Brenda had been such a perfectionist and had talked about how she worked so hard to keep everything in her home neat and tidy and clean, or as much so as possible with three children and a husband. Amy had halfway expected the place to have that look-but-don't touch appearance to it, like a room right out of a magazine or something. But this was a room a person could be comfortable in. Several pairs of rubber boots littered the floor by the sliding glass door to the patio and yard, and rolls of paper—house plans, she assumed, since Riley was a contractor—stood in an umbrella stand next to the largest recliner. Someone was bringing his work home with him these days.

And there, in the center of the middle bookshelf, sat three small ceramic frogs and one larger one, representing Riley and the girls, just as Brenda had described.

"Have a seat anywhere," Riley offered. "Can I get you a cold drink or coffee?"

"Oh, no thank you. Don't go to any trouble on my account. I apologize for not calling before I came."

"Apology accepted but completely unnecessary. You're welcome here any time, and I mean that."

He looked as if he truly did mean it. A funny feeling went through Amy. A little warm, a little fluttery, sending her pulse pounding straight up into her throat. "Thank you," she managed.

Realizing that he wasn't going to sit until she did, she took a seat in the wingback chair. Riley took the large recliner and the girls draped themselves on the arms and his knees and stared at her.

Amy quickly collected herself. "Let's see."

She gave an exaggerated squint as she eyed the three girls. "You," she said to the middle girl, "are Jasmine."

"How'd you know?"

"I think I saw your picture once or twice." *Or three hundred times,* she thought with secret pleasure. "I saw your picture, too," she said to the oldest. "You're Pammy."

"That's right."

"And you," Amy said, eyeing the youngest. "I've seen your picture, too, but your name…is…it's on the tip of my tongue—"

"It's Cindy," the child said with a giggle.

"No, don't help me, I'll get it. Your name is…"

"I told you, it's Cindy."

"No, no, that's not it," Amy told her, frowning and acting distracted.

"Yes, it is. It's Cindy. My name is Cindy."

"No, I'm sure that's not right. I've got it! Esmeralda. Your name is Esmeralda."

Little Cindy squealed with laughter, and so did her sisters. Their father laughed with them.

"Esmeralda, Esmeralda," Pammy and Jasmine sang.

"No, I'm Cindy." The youngest giggled until she hiccuped, then giggled more.

"You know," Amy told Riley as the laughter started to quiet. "I think I might have been wrong. I think she might really be Cindy after all."

He nodded soberly. "I sure hope so, because that's what we've always called her."

"Well, then," Amy said, "we'll just pretend I was wrong and that she really is Cindy. Is that all right?" she asked Cindy.

"Ye-*hic*-okay. Does this mean—" *hic* "—I'm not Esmeralda anymore?"

"Esmeralda, Esmeralda," sang her sisters again.

"I guess not," Amy said. "I'm sorry."

"That's okay," Cindy told her, finally free of the giggles. "I really am Cindy, you know."

"Okay," Amy said. "That's good, then."

The doorbell rang.

Riley eyed his daughters. "Don't you three have a party to go to? I bet that's Marsha, come to walk you to Brandi's."

"Brandi's party!"

"Where's the present?"

"I've got it."

The girls spoke so fast it was nearly impossible for Amy to tell who said what. In the blink of an eye, a gaily-wrapped gift appeared out of nowhere and *whoosh*, they raced to the front door where they met a teenager—Marsha, Amy assumed. Riley spoke a few words to the girl, then the group trailed off down the sidewalk. Suddenly, Amy and Riley were alone.

"Wow," Amy whispered. "Is it like that all the time around here?"

Riley's lips twisted upward. "Welcome to my world." He shrugged. "A birthday party on the next block."

She shook her head slowly. "And here I thought Brenda deserved her medal for the way she died, but now I see she, and you, should have received one for the way you live."

"Medal?" Riley frowned. "Oh, you mean her Purple Heart."

"I mean the other one. The biggie."

"What other one?" he asked slowly.

Amy's stomach sank. "Oh, hell. It hasn't come through yet?"

"What hasn't come through? What are you talking about."

"I can't believe this." Amy clenched her jaw and tried to decide what, if anything, she should say. What if something went wrong and the yahoos in charge decided not to award the medal?

No. She wouldn't let them get away with that.

Neither would the others. "I'm sorry," she told Riley. "I thought it had all been taken care of a long time ago. Brenda was nominated for the Bronze Star."

Riley was sure that he'd heard wrong. "The what?"

"I can't believe this. There must have been a mixup somewhere."

"I don't understand." Riley felt as if a thousand needles were poking the skin of his forearms. "A Bronze Star? Why? It doesn't make any sense."

"Okay." She held a hand up. "Let's start over. What were you told about Brenda's death?"

The words *Brenda* and *death* used in the same sentence no longer knocked the wind out of him as they had a year ago, but there was still pain, so familiar now as to be almost welcome. "Just that she was killed by small-arms fire somewhere around Baghdad."

Amy took a deep breath. "I'm sorry. I thought you knew. Mr. Sinclair, your wife died a hero."

"Hero? Brenda?" His mouth was so dry it was hard to speak. "How? What happened? And don't call me Mr. Sinclair. I'm Riley."

She nodded. "Yes. All right. I'm sorry. I just never dreamed you didn't know." She sighed, then plunged into the story. "We were in a convoy on Route Irish. That's the road between Baghdad and BIOP—Baghdad International Airport. We—our supply unit—had to go to the airport to take personal charge of the incoming shipment because things kept going astray and the colonel was ready to blow a gasket."

Riley swallowed hard. "You and Brenda were in the same unit."

"Yes." Amy rubbed her palms up and down her thighs in a nervous gesture. "On the way back to the city, one of the vehicles ahead of us hit an IED— an improvised explosive device—and all hell broke loose. The morning started out with a Threat Alert Level Amber, and went to Level Black—meaning 'ongoing conflict'—in a heartbeat."

With a storm of emotions rioting through him, Riley listened as Amy told how trucks in front of them exploded and the HumVee Brenda, Amy and others in their unit were riding in had taken so many hits that it quit on them. Bullets were flying at them fast and furious. They were forced to abandon the vehicle and seek cover behind a burned-out tank on the roadside left over from a day or so earlier. One of the guys from the truck behind them ran to join them.

"But there was too much open ground. He took a hit and went down ten yards short of cover."

Riley's stomach rose to his throat. The only reason for Amy to be telling him this was if Brenda...

"Brenda laid down cover fire while Johnson and Cohen went after the wounded private from the other truck. Meeker. Don Meeker. Halfway there, Johnson took one in the leg. Brenda and I left cover and went to help."

Riley forced himself to keep his eyes open, rather than squeezing them shut and covering his ears with his hands to deny what he was hearing.

"It was worse than any nightmare I'd ever had. It was hot and dusty and loud, with smoke from the burning vehicles thick enough to choke a bull elephant. It tasted bitter, the smoke did. Or maybe that was the taste of fear."

She fell silent for so long that Riley nearly choked. Finally he prompted her. "What happened next?"

"What happened next was that Brenda stood out in the open and fired cover, shielding us with her body while Cohen and I got Johnson and Meeker to safety." Amy's eyes grew big and damp and anguished. "She was hit three times, but kept firing cover."

A loud buzzing in Riley's ears threatened to

drown out Amy's words. He struggled to hear, to listen, even as he mentally cheered and simultaneously recoiled from the devastating scene playing out in his mind.

"By the time we made it back to shelter," Amy said quietly, "Brenda had taken a fourth bullet. It was that fourth one—" Her voice broke. "In the throat." She paused again and collected herself. "There was nothing they could do for her. It was too late. I'm so sorry. I didn't mean to come here and stir up old wounds. I'll go now. I'm so sorry." She jumped up to leave.

Riley held out a hand to stop her. "No, wait. Please."

"I never dreamed you didn't know."

"Why wouldn't they have told me? All they said was she was killed by small-arms fire."

Amy sniffed and sat down again. "I guess, technically, that's true. It's just the biggest understatement I've heard lately."

Riley leaned back into his chair. "I can't quite absorb it. Brenda's a...hero? For real?"

"You find that so hard to believe?"

Riley's head snapped up. "No, not at all. It's so typical of her." Suddenly he felt like smiling. "She always was the bravest person I ever knew."

"Really?"

He chuckled darkly. "You haven't met her mother."

Amy surprised him with a laugh. "You mean the Dragon Lady?"

Despite the ache of grief welling up inside him, Riley choked out a bark of laughter. "She told you that?"

Amy smiled. "You may have known her longer but I knew her in the trenches, literally. I might know things about her that you don't. She told me about her mother. She loved her, but she couldn't be the person her mother wanted her to be."

"Something Brenda understood and learned to get around by the time she was in second grade."

"You were close even then?"

"If by close you mean did I live near her, yes, we lived two blocks apart. If you mean *emotionally* close, I was head over heels in love with her before we were out of kindergarten."

Amy smiled. "I can't imagine how she managed to be who she was, and yet please her mother at the same time."

"She developed it into a fine art, but there were times when she couldn't pull it off. Then she had to decide whether to disappoint her mother, or herself."

"It must have been tough to survive on the playground wearing ruffles and lace."

"Especially when she wasn't allowed to get them dirty," Riley clarified. "Her mother would never have forgiven her for getting dirty. Brenda had to keep extra clothes at various friends' houses."

"She was sure resourceful for a child," Amy noted.

"She was desperate," Riley said. "She wanted to do all the things her brothers were allowed to do. She decided to do them behind her mother's back."

"And it hurt them both, because they both knew what was going on."

Riley's chest eased. "You really did know her, didn't you?"

"Yes," she said softly, quietly. "Yes, I did. She was my best friend."

"I don't know what Marva's going to think about your news, but, Frank, Brenda's dad, is going to be so proud, he'll bust his buttons. After he gets over the new rush of grief. What are the chances you can stay in town until they get home from Austin tomorrow and tell them what you just told me?"

"Oh, I don't think—"

"We've got a spare room here," he offered quickly. He didn't want her to leave town yet, but didn't want to cause her any financial hardship, either.

"No, it's not that," she said. "I have a room at the Tribute Inn. But thanks for offering. It's just…are you sure you shouldn't be the one to tell them?"

He shook his head. "Frank will have questions I won't be able to answer. I'd really appreciate it if you'd be the one to tell them. That is, if you can afford the time."

"I've got the time," she told him. "If you want me to talk to them, I'd be glad to. Should I call them tomorrow, or what?"

"Why don't you come for dinner tomorrow evening? I'll get them over here, and the girls can watch TV here in the den while we talk in the living room. How does that sound?"

"Fine. That sounds fine. What about your parents?"

"They moved to Florida years ago. I'll talk to them on the phone."

"Oh," Amy said. "Okay, then. Brenda's parents, dinner tomorrow, here."

Riley relaxed a little more. "Good. Good. Are you sure you wouldn't like something to drink?"

"Oh, no, thanks. I should be going. But there is something I'd like you to think about."

"What's that?" he asked.

"Brenda was putting together some things for the girls for Christmas, you know, last year. When the army packed up her belongings to send home, the gift bags got left behind. I didn't send them right away because they weren't completed. I kept them and worked on them as I could. That's the reason I came here, to give the gifts to the girls. What I need to know from you is, would you rather I give them the gifts now, or wait another three weeks until Christmas?"

"What are the gifts?"

Amy smiled and shook her head. "Surprises. A lot of small things and a couple of larger ones. Tailored to each girl."

"That sounds like Brenda."

"That's right. They're definitely Brenda-type presents."

"You said she meant them to be Christmas presents?"

"Yes."

"Then that's what we'll do."

"Good, because they're still not quite complete. I'll finish them, and if I leave town before Christmas I'll leave the presents with you."

"You're staying in town?"

"For a while. I'll get out of your hair now." She stood and moved toward the door.

Riley rose and followed. "You're not in my hair. You're welcome here anytime, and I mean that, Amy."

"Thank you." At the front door she paused and turned toward him. "She loved you very much."

Riley felt the familiar fist of grief squeeze his heart. "I know. I loved her, too."

Chapter Two

Amy sagged onto the bed in her motel room. She was used to going without food, without sleep. She was used to killing heat, sand in everything including her toothpaste, and total lack of privacy. She'd seen people die. She had shot at men who were shooting at her.

But today, she hadn't done anything that even began to compare to the things she'd been exposed to during the past few years. It was the emotional strain of having to describe Brenda's death to Riley that had drained Amy's reserves. Only the middle of the afternoon, yet all she wanted was to curl into a tight ball and sleep. Seeing no reason why she shouldn't do that very thing, she stripped off her clothes, crawled between the crisp, clean sheets— never again would she take crisp, clean sheets for granted—and was out before she could finish the thought of how lucky Brenda had been to have those three beautiful daughters and that gorgeous hunk of a husband.

Amy slept sixteen hours and woke feeling both ravenous and grungy. A long, hot shower took care of the latter. For the former, she strolled down Main Street in search of a hot meal. But she took her time, ignoring her hunger. She had waited much too long to see and experience the town that Brenda had called home. She'd made it sound so wonderful that for quite some time Amy had thought of it as the hometown she'd never had.

Since it was Sunday and not yet noon, most businesses on Main were closed, but that didn't detract from the appeal of the place for Amy. It was all there, just the way Brenda described. People who smiled and waved, even when they didn't know you. Wide, blue skies. The one and only traffic light.

Just before she reached that light, on the edge

of the town square, the aroma of coffee and bacon wafted beneath her nose and lured her into Dixie's Diner.

It had been a while since she'd eaten in a small café. An American café. The army could, upon occasion, serve up a decent meal now and then, but nothing had ever tasted better to her than the pancakes, bacon and eggs delivered with a smile by a friendly waitress named Nadine.

She ate until she feared she might pop, then resumed her stroll down Main Street. The entire length from one city limits sign to the other was barely a mile. On her way back, she crossed and came down the other side. Once again at the traffic light and the town square, she sat on a bench in the small park before the court house and watched the occasional car go by.

Before she got too comfortable, she got up and strolled to the smallest of the three monuments in the park. Dedicated to the Tribute sons lost not during the Civil War, according to the engraving, but the War Between the States, this smallest monument was divided down the middle. One side was labeled North, the other, South. This being Texas, the names under South far outnumbered those under North.

The next monument was an overall war memorial, listing the Tribute citizens who lost their lives in every war after the Civil War: the Spanish-American War, both world wars, Korea, Vietnam, right up through Desert Storm and Operation Iraqui Freedom. Amy's throat closed. The last name, dated just over a year ago, was Brenda Green Sinclair, Sergeant, U.S. Army.

Amy ran her fingers over Brenda's name. "I'm here, Bren. I brought those presents for the girls. Riley wants to go with your original plan, to give them to the girls for Christmas." She might have said more, but a woman with two children came down the sidewalk from the courthouse.

Amy said a silent goodbye to Brenda and turned away. Across the sidewalk stood the third and final granite monument. This one was named the Tribute Wall. It was more than a simple list of names. Each entry on the twenty-some-foot-long wall told a brief story of an ordinary citizen going above and beyond, and doing something truly heroic. A schoolteacher, Melba Throckmorton, saved her students from a tornado back in 1901. In 1923, unarmed grocer Wendell Stoklosa faced down armed bank robbers to shield a pregnant woman and was shot for his effort.

One after the other were listed, ordinary people putting someone else's welfare above their own, including a man who donated his organs and saved the lives of several people by doing so, and a school janitor rushing the flames to make a daring rescue.

None of those listed were military. Did the powers that be think they didn't belong here because they had their own memorial?

She pursed her lips. All military deaths were not equal. There was getting killed, then there was getting killed because you stepped out and put yourself in harm's way to save someone else. Such an act deserved special recognition, namely, the Bronze Star. And, if Amy could swing it, the Tribute Wall.

Riley's morning did not go as well as Amy's. Neither had his night. His sleep had been plagued with images of his beautiful Brenda playing Rambo on a desert highway. Saving lives. Getting shot on a desert highway. Dying. On a desert highway.

He woke with a silent scream locked in his throat. Never had he had such a dream, one in which he saw her death played out before his mind's eye. Gasping for breath, he glanced at the clock and found it was 4:00 a.m. A trip to the bathroom to splash cold water on his face helped settle him, but he couldn't get those pictures out of his head.

Knowing he wouldn't be able to sleep again that night, he lay in bed and turned on the TV. By 6:00 a.m. he knew all there was to know about roasting anything edible, and three different pieces of exercise equipment, each one the only one he'd ever need.

With his mind sufficiently numbed, he got up and stood under the shower until the numbness cleared and he was able to focus on the day before him. Any day that allowed him to spend time with his three beautiful daughters was a gift, as far as Riley was concerned. If he would rather share that gift with Brenda, that was only natural, but since that was impossible, he wouldn't let missing her take anything away from enjoying the girls. They missed her, too. But every day, he knew that her memory dimmed a little bit more.

That was natural, too, wasn't it? It had to be healthier for them to look ahead and meet each new day with eagerness and excitement than to look back and ache for a loss that could never be recovered. Of course it did.

After having that talk with himself he was able to be completely in the here-and-now for the girls.

After breakfast they drove across town to church and home again.

"I wish Sergeant Amy was here," Cindy said.

All three girls had questioned him repeatedly the evening before. Why had she come? Why had she left? What had they talked about? Was she coming back? Did she talk about Mama? Was she coming back? Why hadn't she stayed? Was she coming back?

It didn't seem to matter how many times he told them that yes, she was coming back, they felt the need to keep asking.

"Are you sure she's coming back?" Pammy asked.

"Okay, that's it." Riley pulled into the garage, but pressed the door lock to seal them all inside the car, then killed the engine. "We're not leaving this car until you girls tell me why you don't believe me when I say she's coming back. Who wants to explain?"

The three girls, strapped in beside each other, shared a look in the backseat of Riley's sedan— the Sunday car, the girls called it, because that's about the only time he drove it.

"Come on." He twisted around to face them. "Just tell me. I'm not going to get mad or anything. Am I?" he thought to add.

"You tell him," Pammy whispered to Jasmine.

"Huh-uh." Jasmine nudged Pammy with her shoulder. "You're oldest."

Pammy grimaced. She frequently played the age card whenever it was to her advantage. This time it was coming back at her. "Okay." She sighed heavily. "It's just that…sometimes you tell us stuff that you know we want to hear, even if it's not real."

Riley's stomach sank. "You think I lie to you?"

"No, Daddy, not on purpose, but sometimes it just happens that way, like with Mama."

He dropped his head to the headrest of his seat and closed his eyes.

"I'm sorry, Daddy. We didn't mean to make you sad."

Riley jerked his head up. "Honey, you didn't make me sad, not the way you think. I'm just sorry that what happened to Mama makes you feel like something bad's going to happen to other people you want to see, like Amy."

"But she's a sergeant, like Mama."

"Yes, she is. But she's right here in Tribute. She spent the night at a motel on Main Street. Wouldn't you think chances are pretty good that she's safe?"

Pammy shared a hopeful look with her sisters. Through their silent "sister" communication, they must have decided to trust his word this time, because they all smiled.

"Okay, Daddy," Pammy offered. "We'll quit asking all the time."

"Good." He smiled. "So, when else have I lied, but not on purpose?"

"When you said you'd think about getting us a puppy."

"I've been thinking about it. I didn't lie, I just haven't decided yet."

"You lied when you said I'd like brussels sprouts," Jasmine claimed.

For the second day in a row, Amy stood at the Sinclair door and rang the bell, only this time she came bearing a half gallon of chocolate chip cookie dough ice cream.

"You may regret this," Riley said as he let her in and took the ice cream from her.

"How so?"

"When the girls see this ice cream, they'll be your slaves for life. This is their favorite flavor."

"Good," Amy said. "Where are they?"

"They're on their way home from their grandparents'. Should be here any minute."

As if on cue, a car pulled up behind Amy's at the

curb. The man behind the wheel honked the horn and three little girls came squealing out of the backseat.

Riley and the man waved at each other, the man gave another toot of his horn, then he drove off.

"Brenda's father?"

"Frank Green. He and Marva will be over after dinner."

If Riley said anything else, Amy didn't hear it over the sound of excited girls.

"You came, you came!"

"Sergeant Amy, you came!"

"Ice cream? You brought us ice cream!"

Dinner with the Sinclairs proved a unique experience for Amy. She had never been the object of such adoration by the three little girls, and something she could only describe as speculation from Riley.

Amy basked in all of it, using it to keep her mind off the coming meeting with Brenda's parents, specifically, her mother, Mrs. Green, who had been dead set against Brenda joining the Guard. Surely Brenda's death must be impossible for her to accept. Now Amy had to bring it all up again, the grief, the anger. She would most likely direct her emotions at Amy.

But Amy could handle it. She had learned a thing or two from Brenda about how to handle her mother and she was ready, as long as she didn't think too much about it beforehand.

Sharing a dinner table with three beautiful, laughing girls trying to outdo each other to entertain her, and their handsome father laughingly keeping order amidst the chaos, did more than take her mind off what was to come.

Handsome father, indeed. Amy had trouble keeping her eyes off him. She felt drawn to him in a way that startled her. It had been a long time since she'd felt such awareness for a man. When their eyes met across the table and held, something earthy and elemental passed between them and gave her a rush.

"I know a joke," four-year-old Cindy announced.

Amy tore her gaze from Riley. "You do?" she asked, trying to focus. The girl seemed a little young to understand the intricacies of timing and punch lines, but, then, Amy didn't know all that much about kids. She winked at Cindy. "Esmeralda knows a joke."

Cindy's eyes widened. She giggled and covered her mouth with her hands. The other two girls giggled, as well, and Riley chuckled.

"No," Cindy snickered. "I'm Cindy."

"Oh, that's right," Amy declared. "I forgot. Sorry. Go ahead, Cindy, tell us your joke."

"Okay. What did one casket say to the other casket?"

Amy glanced at Riley, but the awareness in his eyes made her look away.

"I don't know," she said. "What did one casket say to the other casket?"

Cindy giggled. "Is that you coffin?"

Amy laughed. The joke was funny enough on its own, but the impish look on Cindy's face was even more amusing, making Amy laugh all the harder. "That's a good one, Cindy."

"See?" Cindy stuck her tongue out at Pammy. "I *told* you I could tell a funny joke."

"So?" Pammy wasn't quite sneering, but it was close. "Any imbecile can tell a joke."

"No name-calling," Riley cautioned.

"Yessir," Pammy said.

Cindy waited until Riley looked down at his plate, then made a face at her oldest sister.

Amy swallowed a chuckle.

After dinner, and ice cream for dessert, Amy helped Riley and the girls clean up the kitchen just in time for the arrival of the grandparents.

"Nana! Gramps!" the girls cried when the older couple entered.

Marva Green, Brenda's mother—Nana to the girls—was everything Amy had imagined her to be. Brenda's descriptions had been perfect. Petite, maybe five-two, a hundred and ten pounds, with immaculate makeup and pale-blond hair styled in a sweeping flip. She was dressed in varying shades of pastel pink. Her lipstick and nail polish matched. The only things, including her flesh, that weren't some shade of pink were her blue eyes and lavender eyeshadow. The pink pearl lipstick did nothing to make her smile look genuine.

Nothing, Amy feared, could accomplish that under the present circumstances. The woman was doing great to be able to offer a smile to her grand-daughters. Amy hoped they wouldn't notice the wariness in their grandmother's eyes.

The first thing Amy wanted to do was disarm Mrs. Green. And she knew exactly how to do it. The second Riley said Marva Green's name, Amy reached for the woman's hands and squeezed them. "Oh, I am so glad to finally meet you so I can thank you in person for all those wonderful goodie boxes you sent to the troops in Iraq. Mrs. Green, you were a real lifesaver." Amy knew she was gushing, and it was working; Mrs. Green was smiling. "Even the little things like bobby pins and cotton swabs. But those shampoos and conditioners, and the body lotions. The body lotions nearly caused a riot. We had to draw numbers to see who got them. You were wonderful to think of us that way and go to all that trouble for us."

Marva Green smiled and patted Amy's cheek like a doting grandmother. "I'm so glad you all found a use for the things I sent. I thought it was the least I could do for our brave girls in brown." Suddenly she frowned. "Somehow, that just doesn't have the same ring to it as boys in blue."

"Maybe not," Amy agreed with a smile, "but it's accurate. And you must be Frank Green," she said, turning to Marva's husband.

Frank—Gramps—seemed as genuine as they came. He wasn't a large man, standing maybe five-nine, built of solid muscle. He had the bearing of a man who'd made the armed forces his chosen career for life—straight up, no nonsense. He had the crewcut and salt-and-pepper hair to go with it. He smiled not only with his mouth, but with his eyes.

After the introductions, followed by nearly half an hour with the girls, Riley sent the girls to the den to watch television and give the adults some privacy.

Once they were settled in the living room, Frank Green did what Amy imagined was his habit—he took charge. "Why are we here, Riley? You said there was news about Brenda."

"It was news to me," Riley answered, "but it's something we should have been told when it happened. If not for Amy, we still wouldn't know."

"Know what?" Frank barked.

Riley looked at Amy. "Amy?"

Amy wanted to fidget under the harsh scrutiny of Frank and Marva Green, but she forced herself to sit still. She chose her words as carefully as she could, knowing that Marva Green hated that Brenda had joined the army, and that Frank could not have been happier or more proud. Amy felt as if she were walking a tightrope, trying not to cause any more upset than necessary, but no matter the words she used, this must seem to Marva and Frank like losing their daughter all over again.

"My God," Frank said, stunned by the news Amy delivered. "She should have received the Bronze Star for what she did."

"Yessir," Amy said. "She was nominated. I'm putting in an inquiry to find out the status."

Marva's mouth couldn't have been any tighter. "She's still dead," she said darkly.

"Yes, ma'am," Amy said. "But she's a hero, Mrs. Green."

"Who should have been home tending her babies," Marva spat.

"Mother," Frank growled.

"I know, I know," she said with a sigh. "We are grateful for this information, Miss Galloway, but if you knew her, you had to know how unsuited she was to army life and combat zones and all that dust."

"Forgive me," Amy said. "I know this is upsetting to you, bringing up her death all over again. But you're wrong about Brenda being unsuited. I know you didn't want her there, but she was good at her job. She was a good soldier. She hated being away from her family and her home, but she decided early on that if she was sent to Iraq she would do the best job she could. And she did. She went way above and beyond, and there are four of us who are alive today because of her."

"Correct me if I'm wrong," Marva said, "but it seems to me that if she had stayed under cover she would have been safe. Why couldn't she have just sat still?"

Amy shook her head. "It wasn't in her to let

someone else do what she could do for herself. As for that particular instance, that injured private was a nineteen-year-old kid from Omaha. He'd been terrified all week and trying not to show it. Brenda had taken him under her wing and tried to look out for him. She said he brought out her maternal instincts."

"Sounds just like her," Frank said gruffly. "She was a good girl, our Brenda was. And from what you say, a hell of a soldier."

"That she was," Amy agreed.

"What happened to the private and the other two?" he asked.

"They're okay," Amy said. "A couple of wounds here and there, but nothing vital."

"What about you?" Riley asked quietly.

"What about me?" she asked.

He eyed her steadily. "Were you wounded?"

She waved his question away. "Not so you'd notice."

"What's that mean?" he asked.

"I didn't come here to talk about me. I'm fine."

"Have you been discharged?" Frank asked.

"Yessir," she said.

"How'd you manage that, in this day and age? Usually they're not letting anybody out on time."

"It wasn't on time," she said, "believe me. I

signed up for a one-year hitch in the Guard and ended up serving five. But I'm officially discharged. Until they change their mind and call me back up."

When the Greens were leaving a little while later, Frank shook Amy's hand. "Thank you for telling us what happened. Thank you for being Brenda's friend."

"You're welcome," Amy told him.

Tight-lipped and frosty-eyed, Marva Green gave a sharp nod and stepped outside just ahead of her husband.

"It's times like these," Riley told Amy after the Greens had left, "that I wish I was a drinking man." He eyed her critically. "You look in as bad a shape as I feel. I think we could both use a good stiff drink about now."

"You could be right." Amy felt weak in the knees after the ordeal of telling yet again about Brenda's death.

"I'm afraid the strongest thing I have on hand is beer. Will that do?"

"It'll do fine," she said with a slight smile. "And I don't need a glass."

They took their bottles of ice-cold beer back to the living room. Riley set his down and took a moment to check on the girls before settling on the divan, near the chair that Amy took.

After a long silence, Amy asked, "Will they be all right?"

"The girls?"

"The Greens."

"Eventually."

"I'm afraid I've started the grieving process all over again, for them and for you."

"Maybe," he conceded quietly. "Some."

"I'm sorry." A deep ache of sympathy bloomed in her belly. "I am so sorry."

"You don't have anything to apologize for," he said. "You came here to do a favor for a friend. It's not your fault that the army dropped the ball last year. You shouldn't have had to be the one to tell us how she died. It couldn't have been easy for you, and I made you do it twice. Thank you, Amy."

On the drive home, Marva kept quiet for all of two blocks until she simply couldn't hold her feelings in another second.

"I don't like it, Frank," she stated tightly. "I don't like it one little bit."

Frank pulled slowly away from the stop sign at

Main and turned right. "You don't like that our daughter died a hero?"

Mere mention of her beloved daughter and death in the same sentence still had the power to drain the blood from her brain and her heart. Three slow heartbeats passed before she could speak. "I'm not talking about that. I'm talking about the way Riley looked at that girl."

"What girl? You mean Sergeant Galloway?"

"I mean that Jezebel who sat there and made cow eyes at him while talking about how our baby girl died. Called herself her friend. Ha! And he looked right back, don't you say he didn't, because I saw him." Marva would have gone on, but her chest was heaving, and that was unladylike. If she didn't calm herself, her cheeks would become unattractively flushed, and if she didn't relax her facial muscles, her wrinkles would deepen. God forbid. Some of them, she feared, would soon rival the Grand Canyon.

"So what if he looked back?" Frank asked as he turned into their driveway and hit the button to open the automatic garage door. "He's a red-blooded man, and she's a nice-looking woman. What's wrong with them looking at each other?"

Men, Marva thought with disgust. They just didn't understand a thing. Riley had no business thinking of other women when his own sweet wife had been gone barely more than a year. It wasn't proper.

If Marva had her way, it would never be proper. Riley belonged to Brenda, and always would.

"He's still grieving," she said tersely. "So are the girls. It wouldn't be fair to them for him to bring a new woman into their lives."

"Fair?" His eyes widened, his tone sharpened. "You think it's fair that Riley raise them alone for the rest of his life?"

"He's not raising them alone," she snapped back. "We give him all the help he needs."

"Woman," Frank said with that low growl in his throat that set Marva's back up.

"Don't use that tone with me, Frank Green."

"Don't you go planning Riley's life out for him. Don't think you're going to be the only female those girls have to help raise them. You leave Riley alone when it comes to other women, you hear me? Don't you meddle in his private life."

Marva gave her husband of thirty-eight years a cool glance. She didn't bother arguing with him. She would keep an eye on this Amy girl. If she got too close to Riley and the girls, Marva would have to step in and put a stop to it. The girl couldn't possibly be worthy of Brenda's family.

Chapter Three

Amy could have finished the Christmas presents for the three little girls in a matter of hours and delivered them to Riley Sinclair. Her task would be complete.

But she knew in her heart that she wouldn't. She was going to drag it out as long as possible, because she needed to stay in town long enough to find out if Tribute could become the home she'd never had. She settled into her room at the motel and made herself comfortable.

During the next few days she familiarized herself with the town of Tribute, exploring the shops and city facilities such as the library and courthouse on Main Street. She had sampled the offerings at every restaurant in town and already had a list of two or three favorite meals at each place.

Amy had also done a little research and found out how to go about getting Brenda's name added to the Tribute Wall in the park. She had to write a letter to the city council explaining why Brenda should be added. The mayor's secretary warned her it wouldn't be easy to convince them, because Brenda was already listed on the regular war memorial.

Amy mentally prepared herself for battle. No way was she leaving town now.

The one thing Amy had spent money on since leaving the army was a laptop computer. She didn't waste much on clothes, and her car was as unpretentious—and cheap—as they came. She still had a tidy little sum in savings, so she hadn't minded turning some of it loose for the computer. She was now spending her mornings working on a proposal for the city council to add Brenda's name to the wall.

She was also going to do some in-person politicking. She had learned that the local newspaper publisher, Wade Harrison, had conceived of the wall and seen to its creation. He wasn't on the city council, but even she, who had been out of the country for two years, knew that Wade Harrison had been one of the country's richest, most eligible bachelors and head of one of the country's largest media conglomerates before he'd chucked it all for a woman and a small-town newspaper. The man still had pull. If she could get him on her side, Brenda would be a shoo-in for the wall.

Throughout her exploration of eating places and her effort to get Brenda's name on the wall, and her tinkering with completion of the gifts for the girls, Amy was truly enjoying the town of Tribute. She loved the smallness of it, the fact that everyone seemed to know everyone else. And everyone was so friendly, saying hello whether they knew her or not, asking how she was doing, as if they actually cared.

Every day, Amy felt more and more at home. Her financial situation would allow her to stay in town until the first of the year, but after that she would have to get a job, whether she stayed or moved on.

But before any further heavy thinking could happen, she needed food. It was lunchtime and she was hungry. If she remembered correctly, today's lunch special at Dixie's Diner was spaghetti and meat sauce. She could almost smell it from her motel room.

Ten minutes later she could smell it for real as she followed the Dixie for whom the diner was named and slid into a side booth.

Dixie handed her a menu. "How are you today?"

"I'm fine."

"Can I get you something to drink?"

Amy ordered iced tea and the day's lunch special.

"How nice, you came back."

Amy turned to the elderly woman two tables away, who had introduced herself a couple of days earlier. "Hi, there, Ms. Trotter. Yes, I came back. I couldn't stay away on spaghetti day."

"Neither could I. I can tell you it was worth the trip." There was barely a trace of sauce left on the woman's plate. "And you can call me Ima, dear."

"I'd be honored."

"Miz Ima," came a deep, familiar voice from behind them. "Are you corrupting the visitors to this fine town?"

Ima Trotter pursed her lips and shook a bony finger, but she couldn't hide the twinkle in her eyes. "Riley Sinclair, don't you be giving me a hard time or I'll see to it all the junk mail in town hits your box."

"Yes, ma'am. I take it all back."

"That's much better. Have you made the acquaintance of Sergeant Galloway?"

"Amy, please," Amy said. "I'm not in the National Guard anymore."

"And, yes," Riley offered. "Amy was Brenda's best friend in Iraq, as a matter of fact."

"Well, now, isn't that a wonder. Oh, the stories I bet you could tell."

Dixie returned with Amy's tea, and Ima repeated what Riley had just told her. That exchange took several minutes, during which Ima and a string of men coming from the banquet room in the rear made their way to the cash register.

In the sudden quiet around Amy's booth, Riley looked after Ima as if surprised by something. Slowly he turned toward Amy.

"She's right," he said.

"Pardon?"

"Sorry." He shook his head and smiled. "Hello. How are you?"

Amy chuckled and smiled. "I'm fine. Care to join me?"

"I'd like that. I'd planned to give you a call in the next day or so, to see how you're doing." He slid into the opposite seat of her booth.

How silly for her heart to race just because a man sat across from her. Amy refused to entertain the notion that her reaction was specific to this particular man. For Heaven's sake, this was Brenda's husband.

She took a sip of tea, then wiped her palms on her thighs. "I just ordered. Have you eaten?"

"Yeah." He nodded toward the banquet room. "Back there. Monthly Chamber of Commerce lunch."

"You're a member?"

"My company is. Sinclair Construction."

"I'm impressed."

He chuckled. "Don't be. All you have to do is pay dues to belong."

Amy didn't have a comeback for that. The small silence played on her nerves.

"I wanted to ask…" Riley began.

She'd been so deep in thought that his voice startled her and made her jump. "Oh—sorry. My mind wandered. You wanted to ask?"

"It was something Ima said, about stories."

"What about them?"

"Could you? I mean, could you tell stories about Brenda in Iraq? Not about that last day, or bullets or bombs or any of the other terrifying things I'm sure you saw, but other things. What it was like to live in a foreign land. Maybe funny stuff my girls would enjoy hearing about their mother. Is there anything like that you can tell them?"

Amy puffed out her cheeks and exhaled. "Whew. That's…"

"Too much?"

"No," she said thoughtfully. "It's a great idea. Brenda would love that you thought of it, and it would go along with, well, other elements of their Christmas gifts."

"What other elements?"

She flashed him a smile. "Never mind that."

"Spoilsport," he muttered with half a smile. "Let's not make this about Christmas, if you've got something similar going there."

"What do you have in mind?"

He glanced at his watch and winced. "I'm a little short on time right now. If you're serious about the stories, what about telling them to the girls, and I can videotape it so they can play it back whenever they want to?"

"That sounds like a great idea."

"If you're free this evening, you could come over and we can figure out the logistics."

Amy's pulse raced. "All right. What time do you want me?"

Something flared in his eyes, and she realized what she'd said.

"Uh, to show up," she finished quickly, wondering if she'd read more into that look than had really been there.

Dixie arrived with a steaming plate of spaghetti. "Here you go. Enjoy."

"Thanks, Dixie."

When the waitress left, Riley said, "You've made some friends."

"A few," she acknowledged.

"Can you come for supper tonight? Around six?"

"Only if you let me help."

"You can make the salad. I have all the ingredients."

"Sounds like a deal."

He left then, and Amy felt…deflated? Was that the right word to describe the empty feeling now that a great deal of warmth and enjoyment had just left the café?

Riley climbed into his pickup and swung by his office to pick up the plans for the Wilson job. He'd known Bob Wilson since second grade, and this was the man's first new home. He'd entrusted his dream to Riley, who intended to make certain that trust was not misplaced. His crews were always good, but there was no substitute for a little first-hand oversight.

The plans were right where they were supposed to be. Everything in his office was, but that didn't mean it didn't look like a trash pit. He was an outstanding builder. He was not a great office manager. He'd had a so-so secretary until a couple of months ago, but when she got pregnant with her third child she decided to stay home. Since then he'd been making do.

He really should hire someone.

At least worrying about his office took his mind off Amy Galloway. Or it had, until how.

He found it disconcerting to have a woman other than Brenda pop up in his mind every time he turned around. Especially when the woman doing the popping was Brenda's best friend from the army. He couldn't think of anything more inappropriate.

In his rational mind, he knew Brenda was dead. He wasn't one of those people who tiptoed around and said she was *gone* or *no longer with us* or *passed on* or any of the other dozen or more euphemisms people used to avoid admitting that someone had died.

And now he felt drawn to the woman who'd brought him the truth of his wife's death.

He knew there was nothing wrong with being interested in a woman, even this woman. He'd been alone more than a year now. To feel guilty was ridiculous. Yet guilty was exactly how he felt.

"Jackass," he muttered to himself as he grabbed the Wilson plans and locked the door on his way out. It wasn't as if he was going to jump her bones or anything. He was merely going to videotape her telling stories to his girls.

She danced around in his mind all afternoon until genuine anticipation built up inside him. So did his guilt.

After leaving the Wilson job site Riley drove to the Greens' to pick up the girls. Regardless of the lifelong tension between Marva and him, Riley was the first to admit that she had been a godsend to him and his daughters since Brenda's death. The Green house sat directly across the street from the elementary school, so the girls went there every afternoon and stayed until Riley picked them up. Cindy, whose pre-kindergarten let out at noon, spent the most time with her nana.

That was starting to show, too, and it concerned Riley. Cindy didn't appear to have as strong a personality as Brenda had had at that age. Not that he remembered Brenda from pre-school, but he had strong memories of her in first grade, and by then she'd already been well on her way to understanding how to get her own way yet still honor her mother's wishes.

Marva Green fancied herself a Southern belle, and had raised—or tried to raise—her daughter to be ultra feminine. In many ways Marva had succeeded. Brenda was forever draped in ruffles and lace, frills on everything, everything matching everything else, and those fat sausage curls bouncing down her back with every graceful move she made.

But Brenda had wanted to play softball and soccer, basketball and volleyball, and her favorite color was red. She'd had to fight Marva from the beginning for the right to play sports, because according to Marva, proper young ladies did not get dirty, nor did they partake of any activity that caused them to—oh, hideous thought!—perspire.

Brenda had learned the manners her mother insisted upon, and she had made sure she looked beautiful and remained mostly silent. Unless she wanted to do otherwise. On those occasions, she simply dressed as she pleased, smiled at her mother and went on her way.

It had always amazed him how Brenda could smile so cheerily in the face of her mother's fiercest, scariest frown. The woman could be downright frightening, yet Brenda had never been afraid. She hadn't enjoyed going against her mother's wishes, but she never wanted to lose herself to Marva's idea of femininity.

Now Cindy was talking about ruffles and bows and frills, and Riley didn't know how to tell if she really liked those things or if she was just trying to please her nana. Of course, Pammy and Jasmine liked pretty dresses, too, but they had never wanted to wear them every day the way Cindy suddenly did.

When he pulled up in the driveway, he played coward and honked his horn. A moment later the girls trailed out of the house, dragging overcoats and backpacks behind them. Marva called them all back to the porch for a goodbye kiss, then frowned at him as they traipsed to the truck.

Riley decided to take a page from Brenda's book. He smiled at Marva and waved, as if he had no idea she disapproved. *A gentleman always comes to the door to pick up a lady.* Or in this case, three.

Instantly his pickup echoed with little-girl chatter. In the short trip home he learned every important thing that had happened that day at Tribute Elementary. The chattering and giggling, even the arguing, was music to his ears. Especially the squeals of delight when he told them Amy was coming to supper and afterward would tell them a story about their mother.

Brenda, thank you for sending Amy for the girls. They needed whatever pieces of their mother Amy could provide. Riley tried to tell them as much as he could, but Amy knew a part of Brenda that he didn't. He was probably more eager to hear about it than the kids.

The doorbell surprised him. He wasn't ready. He'd wanted to clear her out of his mind before facing her again. Too late now.

"It's Sergeant Amy," Pammy called from the front hall.

He heard Amy answer, heard Jasmine and Cindy chime in. Laughter. Giggles.

Riley washed his hands at the kitchen sink, and,

still drying them, sauntered to the front hall to greet their guest. "You made it. Great."

"We're making supper." Pammy took Amy by the hand and led her to the kitchen. "But you don't have to help, you can just watch, 'cause you're company."

Riley saw Amy open her mouth to protest and jumped in to clarify. "Oh, no," he protested. "She has to help. I told her she had to if she wanted to eat. She can toss the salad while you three set the table."

"But, Daddy, she's company. Why are you making her work?"

"He's teasing," Amy said. "I made him promise to let me help so I wouldn't feel like a freeloader. Do you know what a freeloader is?"

"A moocher," Jasmine proclaimed.

Amy chuckled. "That's right. And I didn't want to be a moocher. If you guys are going to feed me, I want to help put the dinner together."

And so she did. It got a little confusing with five people crowding into the kitchen, and even more so because Cindy wanted to help everybody, consequently hindering everyone.

He watched Amy as she tore the lettuce, diced tomatoes, cubed the three hard-boiled eggs he had set aside for the salad, all the while stepping this way and that to make room for or get out of the way of one or more of the girls. She seemed so natural around them.

"I never asked," he said quietly. "Have you ever been married?"

"Who, me? No. Do you want the carrot grated or sliced?"

"Grated. Do you have any kids of your own?"

"No, no kids."

At the dining-room table, an argument broke out between Pammy and Jasmine over who was in charge.

Riley rolled his eyes. "Want some?"

Amy laughed. "Are you kidding? You wouldn't trade your girls for anything. You're crazy about them. A blind man could see that."

He chuckled. "I guess so. I guess I kinda like having them around."

"Before I forget," Amy said, "did you mean to invite the Greens to hear these stories you want me to tell?"

He didn't answer right away. He wanted to give the illusion that he was at least considering the idea. "No," he finally said. "Not this time."

"Are you sure? You know they would love to hear anything to do with Brenda."

"I know. But now and then I'd like the girls to

have a piece of their mother that everybody else doesn't have. Something that belongs just to them."

She met his gaze for a long moment, then shrugged. "It's your decision."

"Yes, it is."

Amy found this second supper with the Sinclairs as much fun and as laughter-filled as the first. Except for that one little cloud. She shouldn't have opened her mouth about inviting the Greens for what the girls were calling Story Time. Riley was right, it wasn't her business. She had crossed a line she hadn't realized was so important to him.

She'd known from Brenda that her mother wasn't Riley's favorite woman, but she also knew that he relied on Marva Green for help with the girls.

But Amy had obviously hit a nerve earlier by asking about including his in-laws, or former in-laws, whatever they were. Riley had been all but ignoring her throughout supper by never looking her in the eye.

But they made it through the meal, and through the cleanup after, and gradually he seemed to thaw a little. Still, even standing next to him at the sink, she felt a distance that hadn't been there before.

Okay, that was fair. They were nearly strangers. Their connection was his late wife. That had brought them closer at a speed faster than normal. Then she had presumed to suggest how to share memories of Brenda, as if she had a right.

The distance he put between them now, when she thought about it, seemed more appropriate than the emotional pull she had been feeling. She told herself to get comfortable with it, and her private pep talk felt as if it was working. By the time they finished cleaning up she felt at ease.

Or, she would have, if he hadn't rolled his sleeves up and exposed his forearms while rinsing the dishes. They were the forearms, and hands, of a man who used them to earn his living.

Who knew the mere sight of a man's forearms could be so arousing? They were strong and thick and tanned, with a dusting of dark hair that made her want to stroke it with her fingers.

And his hands. Wide-palmed, with long, deft fingers. Making her wonder what they would feel like against her flesh.

Mercy. If she didn't get her mind off sex she was going to spontaneously combust right there in his kitchen. She turned away from him and saw three little girls carrying the last of the dishes from the table and reminded herself that she was here for them. Not to jump their daddy's bones.

When the cleanup was over, Riley announced that he wanted to tape the storytelling in the girls' bedroom.

"Yea!" The girls cheered and bounced up and down.

Then little Cindy grabbed Amy's hand and tugged her toward the hall. "C'mon, Sergeant Amy, I'll take you. You'll like it. Daddy even made us clean it before you came."

"That was lucky," Jasmine claimed.

Amy chuckled. "I bet it wasn't that messy to start with."

"You'd be wrong," Riley said. "It looked like a giant laundry and toy dump."

"Oh, Daddy." Pammy wrinkled her nose.

"Oh, Pammy." Riley brushed his finger across the tip of said nose as he mimicked her giggly tone.

The girls shared the large front corner bedroom. Somehow, three twin-sized beds and three small dressers fitted, leaving ample room for toys and space to play with them. Sheer pink-and-white ruffled curtains covered the two windows, but there any unity in color and style ended.

Cindy tugged her through the door. "This is my

bed." She raced across to the bed farthest from the door and bounced her little rear on its pink-flowered quilt with a pink-and-white ruffled pillow sham and matching dust ruffle. A little girl's fairy-tale bed.

In the far corner, near the foot of Cindy's bed, sat an old wooden rocker.

"That's Jasmine's bed, the yellow one in the middle," Cindy said. "'Cause she's the middle sister, and the blue bed by the closet is Pammy's. She likes blue. A lot."

"She does, huh?"

"Oh, yes," Cindy asserted. "You're gonna tell us a story?"

"I thought I would, if you want."

"Sit here." Cindy patted the smooth oak seat of the rocker. "It's our story chair."

Amy had a sudden picture of Brenda sitting in this very chair, holding one of these beautiful darlings to her breast to nurse. Another followed, of Riley holding a crying baby in the middle of the night while Brenda slept down the hall. The chair took on sacred proportions in her mind. She looked to Riley, wondering if she had the right to even touch that chair.

He, of course, looked oblivious to the emotions suddenly swamping her. "Go ahead, have a seat. I want to set the video camera up over here. Girls, you can sit on the end of the bed, or on the floor in front of Amy."

"Do we get to be in the video, too?" Jasmine asked.

"Of course," he said, as if no other way would do. "What is a video without my three best girls?"

Pammy blinked up at him. "Blank tape?"

"Oh, a smartypants," he said darkly.

"Not me," Pammy denied.

Jasmine crawled onto the foot of Cindy's bed and sat crosslegged while Riley set up a tripod between Pammy and Jasmine's beds for his camera.

Pammy nudged Jasmine. "Move over."

Jasmine moved over and Pammy joined her.

"Hey," Cindy cried. "You guys got my bed."

"Sit on the floor," Pammy said.

Cindy looked as if her oldest sister had suggested she sit in the middle of the train tracks with the train on the way.

Before the outrage on that pretty little face could erupt, Amy sat in the rocker and took Cindy's hand. "Would you like to sit on my lap?"

Cindy's entire face lit up. "Can I? Can I?" Without waiting for a yes or no, she climbed onto

Amy's lap and beamed up at her with a bright-eyed smile. "Like this?"

Amy felt a thick lump emerge in her throat. Without thinking, she slipped one arm around the girl's back. "Exactly like this."

"That's good." Riley leaned down and looked through the camera lens. "Just like that. Is everybody comfortable?"

"Yes," they all said.

"Okay, then." He straightened and smiled. "Amy, whenever you're ready."

"Oh." Suddenly she felt the need to wipe the dampness from her palms, but she had a four-year-old in her lap. She addressed herself to the girls. "Your dad thought you might like to know what things were like for your mom in Iraq."

"Yeah."

"Yes."

"Tell us."

"Okay," she agreed. "Is there anything in particular you want to know?"

"What did she do for fun?" Jasmine wanted to know.

"Hmm. Let's see." Amy thought a minute. "Okay, fun. The army has a place, like a big room, and it's got computers so we can get online, treadmills for working out, video games, television. All that kind of stuff. One of the things your mom liked best was reading. Your nana and a lot of other people sent paperback books and we had this lending-library thing going where a big group of us swapped books with each other. Your mom loved to read those books. She said she could tune everything else out and live inside those stories and know that, in the end, everything was going to work out. And the room where she went to read, the one with the computers and everything, had air conditioning."

Mention of air conditioning didn't faze the girls, but Riley caught on, she noticed, and from there Amy moved on to tell the girls about the heat and the dust and sand of the desert. The girls made ugly faces and gagging noises at the idea of sand in their teeth, sand in their sheets, sand in their shoes. They laughed at the thought of having to stand in a bucket to take a bath, which any number of female military personnel had to do when away from better facilities for too long.

"One of the things your mom missed the most, along with her friends and family and air conditioning, was cottonwoods. They have all kinds of trees over there. Willows and alders and locust, and, of course, the date palms. Your mom really liked the date palms. But she used to talk about the cottonwoods that line a creek at the edge of town back home. The way she described them, with their bright green leaves, their particular scent, especially when they start turning yellow in the fall—if you closed your eyes and listened to her talk about them, you could swear you were sitting under one, hearing the rustle of the leaves, smelling that pungent tang, feeling the coolness of their shade."

Lost in the memory of one of Brenda's cottonwood descriptions, with her eyes closed, Amy inhaled and smelled the very scent she'd been describing and for a moment, forgot where she was.

Riley, too, felt himself getting lost. Bypassing the small screen on his camera, he looked through the lens and focused in on Amy's face. It was as if a sudden connection formed between them, even though they were separated by eight feet of room and her closed eyes. Between his eyes and her face, nothing separated them but the camera lens.

"But the single thing she missed," Amy said in a low, smooth voice that sounded to Riley like a woman seducing her lover, "more than any other thing, besides you and the rest of her family and friends, was green grass."

"Grass won't grow there because it's a desert, right?" Jasmine guessed.

"Part of it's a desert, that's right, but a great big part of it is lush and green and can grow anything, when the irrigation is working. But we never got to see much of that part. She said she missed being able to take off her shoes and dig her bare toes into cool, green grass. She missed the smell of it when it was freshly mowed."

Amy closed her eyes again while she spoke, and, seeing her face close-up in the lens, Riley could practically feel the cool grass, smell the fresh clippings.

With his attention centered on her, he saw her in a clear light, in a way he hadn't before. No evasions, no ignoring. No comparing her to another. She wasn't a soldier, wasn't even Brenda's best friend. There were no beautiful daughters, no in-laws, not even a late wife. For this one startling instant, in his vision, there was only Amy.

Chapter Four

The next afternoon, when Amy returned to her motel room from a long walk after lunch, a message awaited her. Riley had called and left a number and a request for her to call him back.

Amy sat on the side of her bed and stared at the phone. Last night something had happened. She'd been thinking about it all day and had yet to figure it out. One minute she'd been telling the girls about Brenda missing cottonwoods and grass, the next, Riley had been showing her to the door.

She could only assume that hearing so much

about Brenda had stirred up old memories and grief, and he had suddenly needed to be alone.

Amy ached for him and prayed that the girls had not suffered the same reaction. They hadn't seemed sad. They had seemed curious and interested in what she had to say about their mother. Of course, at their ages, Brenda wasn't as real to them anymore as she was to Riley. His entire life with her must seem like yesterday.

He was surely calling to tell her he didn't want her to tell any more stories to his girls. But she had to return his call despite the dread stirring in the pit of her stomach. To ignore his message would be rude.

Come on, soldier up, Galloway.

Squaring her shoulders, Amy reached for the phone and dialed the number.

A woman answered. "Sinclair Construction." A frazzled woman, by the sound of her.

Just as Amy was about to speak she heard a loud crash over the line, followed by a low, male curse in the background and a moan and a *tsk* from the woman on the phone.

"Is everything okay?" Amy asked.

"What? Oh, yes, I'm sorry. Just a slight mishap. What can I do for you?"

"I'm returning Mr. Sinclair's call."

"Oh, dear, hold on."

"If now's not a good time—"

"No, no, just let me get him."

Instead of using the hold button, the woman must have simply laid the phone on the desk. Amy heard papers rustling. The woman shouted for Riley to get the phone. He shouted something back. A door slammed.

Had he left?

He yelled something again. He hadn't left.

"With any luck," the woman said in a none-too-friendly tone, "it's someone who wants to come to work here and clean up this mess."

Heavy bootsteps. He grumbled something that sounded like, "I should be so lucky." More papers rattled. Then a harsh breath. "Hello?"

"Riley?"

"Amy?"

"Yeah, it's me. Sounds like you're busy."

"Oh, just a little." There was laughter in his voice. "What can I do for you?"

"I don't know. You called me, asked me to call back?"

"Oh, hell. Sorry. I forgot."

"Look, you've obviously got your hands full

right now. Why don't we touch base later when you've got more time?"

"If I don't find someone to make sense out of the mess in my office, I may never have time. But I was calling to say thank you for last night."

Amy heard a definite hoot of laughter followed by "Hallelujah!" from somewhere near Riley.

"Oh, hell," he muttered.

Amy couldn't help it. She laughed. "You stepped into that one, didn't you?"

"Fanny, that's not—"

"Good for you, Riley," Fanny said with a laugh. "It's about damn time."

"Amy, I apologize for the static in the background." He sounded as if he was grinding his teeth. "I wanted to thank you for the time you spent with my daughters last night, telling them those stories about their mother. After you left it took forever to get them to bed, they were so excited."

Amy felt the muscles across her shoulders relax. He was thanking her. She hadn't expected that. "You don't need to thank me, Riley. I loved doing it. Your girls are terrific. I see why Brenda was so proud of them. She would be proud of you, too, for the way you've raised them without her here to help."

He didn't answer.

"Riley?"

"I'm sorry. You, ah, left me speechless."

"Is that good or bad?"

"In this case, it's good. Thank you. That was the nicest thing anyone's said to me in a long time. Most people tiptoe around Brenda when they talk to me. They act as if she never existed. Like if they mention her name I'm going to crumble."

"Some people are uncomfortable with the idea that we all die, and don't know how to talk about it. Or maybe they're afraid you can't handle the reminder so soon. Or something. Whatever, it's a shame."

"All the tap-dancing is what makes me uncomfortable. Thank you for not tap-dancing."

"I wouldn't look good in a tutu."

"I bet you would, but I thought a tutu was for ballet."

"Whichever. Soldiers don't wear tutus. I'm sure there's a rule."

"Ah, but you're not a soldier anymore."

"Yeah." She heaved a sigh. "I'm not."

"Feeling a little lost, are you?"

"Not me. Until you fire me, I have meaningful work."

"Beg pardon? You work for me?"

"I tell stories to your daughters."

"Ah, I see. Listen. You've just given me a wild idea. Do you have time this afternoon to get together and talk?"

"Today?"

"Yeah, today, like in about twenty minutes."

"Oh, I don't know, Riley. Jamie is supposed to have her baby this afternoon, and Mick's getting out of prison, but he doesn't know the baby is his, and Erica is going to try to steal Marco's sperm from the sperm bank. I'm not sure I can give all that up for you."

"Uh…"

"Oh, what the heck. I'll see you in twenty."

"Okay, then. Twenty minutes."

It was a crazy idea, Riley acknowledged, but he couldn't get it out of his head, so he was going to run with it. All she could do was laugh in his face, and she probably wouldn't do that. She would simply turn him down if she didn't go for it. Or maybe she would think she wasn't qualified, or overqualified, or—

Hell. He pulled into the motel parking lot. Too late now. There she stood, in her worn jeans and Go Guard sweatshirt, which was all the coverup she needed on this fifty-degree December day.

"Hi." She climbed into his pickup.

"Hi. You sure you don't mind missing what's-her-name's baby?"

She laughed. "I'd never even watched that soap until two days ago, so I guess I'll live if I have to give it up."

"What a trooper."

"Not anymore. I've been discharged."

"So you have." He turned off onto the road to Wilson's new place. "You don't mind riding out to a job site with me, do you?"

"Of course not."

"Good. So now that you're discharged, what do you want to do with yourself? Where are you going to live?"

"I haven't decided. That's the reason I'm still here."

"Here?" Oh, yeah. "You're thinking of living in Tribute?"

"Why does that surprise you?"

With his gaze on the road in front of him, he shrugged. "It's just that few people actually move here. Most people move away."

"If that were true, this would be a ghost town by now."

"Okay, a slight exaggeration. But why pick Tribute? You could live anywhere."

"The fact that I can live anywhere I want is why I'm here. I guess I've loved it here since those terrible, hot nights in the desert, when I begged Brenda to talk about something, anything. Brenda talked about Tribute and how much she loved it. I mentally adopted the town. I've never lived in one spot longer than a few months, always being shuffled from one relative to another while my mother took off for parts unknown."

"What about your father?"

She shrugged. "Never met the man. I'm not sure my mother knows who he is. I never thought to myself, 'I wish I had a dad, or a mom who stayed put.' It wasn't parents I always wanted, it was a home. A hometown. For more than a year I've held Tribute in my mind, and now, here I am."

"Wow. That's quite a lot for a little town like Tribute to live up to."

"On the contrary. It's everything I dreamed it would be."

"So you're sticking around?"

"I'm sticking. I need to put down roots. Do you

realize that I lived in Iraq longer than I've lived anywhere in my life? That's pitiful. Oh, yeah, I'm here and I'm sticking."

"Okay, then. I don't mean to get too personal, but how long can you hang around without needing a job?"

"If it was anybody but you asking, I wouldn't answer that, but because it's you…I can make it until the end of the year, but then I'll need a job, no matter where I am."

Riley turned into the drive and parked beside the roofer's truck.

"Is this one of your jobs?" Amy asked, eyeing the house in progress.

"Yes. Three thousand square feet of living space, three-car garage, covered patio, in-ground pool, barn, tool shed, cross-fencing. He wants us to do it all. Or rather, his wife does. He keeps saying he'll hire somebody to do the outdoor items, but his wife says no, I have to do them because Bob will never get around to it and she'll be an old woman before she gets to swim in the pool."

"Ah, a woman who knows her man."

"That she does," he said. "Maryann has known Bob as long as I knew Brenda—since around first grade."

"So maybe not everybody leaves town?"

"I'd say about half go, half stay."

"And some come from somewhere else," she said. "Sounds about normal to me."

"Could be. You want to be one of the ones who moves here from somewhere else."

"Looks like it."

"I've got to check on a couple of things here." He reached for the door handle.

"May I come with you?"

He paused and looked at her, pleased by her request. "Sure, if you want."

They climbed from his pickup and she followed him into the open garage of the new house, where the roofer was taking a break with a cold can of pop while he thumbed through a pile of wrinkled invoices.

"Hey, Red. This is a friend of mine, Amy Galloway. Amy, Red Conklin, my favorite roofer."

"Ma'am."

They talked for a few minutes, until Riley was satisfied that the roof would be finished by dark that evening. "All right, then. That'll be great. I'll hold you to it."

Riley showed Amy around the inside of the house. Twice his cell phone rang, potential cus-

tomers wanting estimates. That the calls were for-
warded to his cell told him Fanny had closed up
and gone home for the day.

What did people do without cell phones?

He finished the second call and glanced around
inside the house. "With the roof finished and the
doors installed, we can start putting in the drywall,
then the woodwork, the fixtures, and before you
know it, it'll be a finished home. What are you
smiling about?"

"You," she said. "You enjoy your work. I like
that."

He shook his head and steered her back out to
his pickup. "I like this part of my work."

"This part?"

"Anything that's done out of the office."

"Ah, I see."

"Not yet, but you will."

Amy had yet to figure out why Riley had called
her. He'd said he had something he wanted to talk
to her about. But she didn't ask him about it now
as they turned back onto Main, because she was
enjoying the ride, the sights of the town. The fresh
air. Riley's company.

Never mind the latter, she told herself. She

didn't trust her own emotions where Riley was concerned. She feared that her feelings for him were like her feelings for the town—virtually in place before she came to town because of Brenda's stories. Half in love before first sight.

For a town, that was fine. For a man, it was disaster.

The man in question turned into a driveway and parked before a small, neat, redbrick building attached to the front of a large metal warehouse. The sign on the front door and another stretched along the side of the warehouse read Sinclair Construction.

"Wow," Amy said. "I thought you worked out of a trailer house."

"I outgrew it shortly after Brenda shipped out."

"Did she know about it?" Her husband moving into a larger space, and a location on Main Street, was the kind of news Brenda would have shared. She would have bragged about it to one and all.

"No. I didn't move in here until after her funeral. I should have done it sooner, but I was waiting for her to come home that fall. I didn't want to make a move like that without her being here."

"But in the end, you had to."

He killed the engine and looked at her. "I outgrew the old place. It was either move and grow, or strangle and suffocate."

Amy's heart gave a heavy *thud* behind her ribs. For a moment she thought she saw a hidden message in his eyes, but he blinked and whatever she thought she'd seen disappeared.

She looked away and studied the building. "What was here before you?"

"A drilling supply company."

"Drilling, as in Texas tea?"

"Black gold," he agreed. "The whole town was pleased when they outgrew this site and built a new, larger place at the edge of town. A good bit of our economy depends on the oil industry. They do good, the town does good. The town does good, Sinclair Construction does good. Come on. I'll show you around."

Why, she wondered. Why did he want her to see his office? But she wasn't quite ready to ask. She figured he would explain himself soon enough. For now she would simply enjoy his company. Questions could come later.

The front door of the business was locked; Riley had to use his key to let them in. "You don't have full-time office help?" she asked.

"Not yet. Fanny comes in a few hours a week and takes care of the bookkeeping. Sort of."

Amy chuckled at his dire tone. "How's that working for you?"

"Hmph. Not well. You want a job?"

She laughed. When he didn't, she gave him a closer look. He didn't appear to be kidding. In fact, he looked, if anything, hopeful. "Are you serious?"

"As a heart attack," he said. "In fact, that's what I wanted to talk to you about today."

"You want me to be your what, secretary? Receptionist? I don't know anything about those jobs."

"That's not what I need. I need someone who can order supplies, keep track of the different crews, where they're supposed to be, and when they need to be there. Pay the bills. I need a combination job juggler, supply manager, and drill sergeant, with a little phone-answering thrown in."

"In other words, everything but bookkeeping," she offered.

"That's it. You interested?"

Amy looked around the outer office, with its two desks, one fairly neat, the other a mess of paperwork, a box of ink pens, two unopened reams of copier paper, and a power screwdriver.

Her hands tingled with eagerness to attack the

mess and make order of it. "You're offering me a job?"

"I'm offering you a job. I don't want you to feel obligated to take it because of Brenda. This is just me offering a job to you. I need an office manager, somebody to do everything I don't have time to do."

"Or don't want to do?"

A small smile flashed across his face. "That, too."

The salary he offered wouldn't make her rich, but it was more than she'd expected. She doubted anyone else in town would offer her a job she wanted, that she felt supremely capable of doing, for more money.

Besides, if she worked somewhere else, she wouldn't get to see Riley every day. Here, she would. That was both the good news and the bad. But she was willing to suffer through being in his company every day. What a hardship.

She smiled and held her hand out to shake, "Is this my desk? When do I start?"

Amy showed up for work promptly at eight-thirty the next morning. Not one to worry much over her own looks, but with a nod toward "business attire," albeit a construction business with a boss who wore denim and flannel to the office, she wore a white shirt with her blue jeans. Practically formal attire, in her book, but she decided it wouldn't be too much for the first day on the job. She drew the line, however, at tucking in her shirttail.

Riley was already in the office when she entered. He sat behind his desk in the far alcove—not really a separate room, but definitely separate—with the phone to one ear while he murmured incomprehensible phrases and scribbled numbers and abbreviations on a notepad. His day had obviously already started.

After hanging her coat next to his on a hook by the front door, she sat at her desk and checked the drawers for space to keep her bag. She found stacks of both new and used file folders, an adding machine with the electrical cord wrapped around it, boxes of pencils and pens, mostly unopened, and one drawer set up with hanging folders, all empty. She found lots of things, but no space large enough for her bag.

It would have fitted neatly in with the adding machine—for that matter, the adding machine didn't belong in a desk drawer, but she didn't see anyplace else to put it for now—if she carried a regular purse, even a large purse. But she was so used to carrying a backpack that she had yet to give it up in civilian life.

She crammed her bag beneath the desk, then took inventory of the desktop. More stacks of supplies, those same piles of rumpled forms she'd seen yesterday, a black two-line phone, the power screwdriver she'd noticed the day before, and a computer bearing a nice layer of dust.

Across the room stood the other desk, all neat and tidy, no large stacks of anything. Fanny's desk. Next to it, on a wheeled stand, stood a fancy laser printer. In another corner sat a copier. A short hall led to the warehouse area behind the office building, with one door on either side, perhaps for restroom and storage. In Riley's area were several file cabinets, shelves on the walls, rolls of what looked like architectural plans, and a fax machine.

Riley finished his phone conversation and hung up. He stood and smiled. "Good morning. Welcome to Sinclair Construction."

Amy's pulse gave a little leap. She told it to stop such nonsense even as she smiled back at Riley. "Good morning. And thank you."

"I—" The phone rang. "Excuse me."

She supposed she should be answering the phone, but Riley didn't give her the chance.

"Maryann, what's wrong? What do you mean, it's all wrong? What's all wrong? You're out at the house now? Okay, just sit tight. I'll be there in ten minutes."

He hung up, grabbed the plans and his keys from the desk.

"Problems?" Amy asked stupidly.

"I don't know. Maryann's out at that house I showed you yesterday, claiming the walls are all wrong." He grimaced as he took a key from his key ring. "Here. This is your key to the front door."

When he placed it in her hand, the key was warm and so was his touch. Their eyes met and locked. For a long moment they stood that way, as if frozen, yet there was nothing resembling cold in the room.

Finally he let his fingers slide from her hand and took a step backward. "If you leave for lunch or at the end of the day, make sure the door into the warehouse is locked from this side. Not that I'll be gone all day. Sorry to leave you here like this your first day. Just poke around if you want."

With his gaze still locked on hers, he placed a hand on the doorknob. "I don't know when I'll get back, but Fanny should be in around one or so. She can answer a lot of questions about this place. Will you be all right?"

"I'll be fine." *If I find enough air to breathe.*

"All right," he said. "See you later."

He stood there holding her gaze for another moment before finally turning away. Then it was as if someone fired the starting gun of a race. He jerked open the door and left in a rush of sound and air, leaving a vacuum in his wake.

Amy stood in the middle of the office and simply breathed for a couple of minutes, then snapped out of it and set to work. By the time she realized she was hungry, she checked the clock on the wall and was surprised to see it was lunchtime.

Hands on her hips, she stood and glanced around. The main office—hers and Fanny's—looked much better. The dust was gone, and the piles of paperwork were sorted into those heretofore-unused hanging folders. The spare equipment now sat on the bottom shelf in Riley's office. The CPU of her computer system had a nice spot on a low stand beside her desk in a protected area where the cables wouldn't be in the way.

All that was left on her desk now were her monitor, keyboard, mouse with pad, notepad, telephone, a calculator she'd found in the closet to replace the big, old adding machine that had been in her desk, and a tall cup for pens and pencils.

Now it was time for lunch. She slipped into the restroom to wash her hands. As she was coming out, the front door opened. The woman who entered looked to be in her seventies, with iron-gray hair pulled back in a loose bun, with loose frizzy curls around her face. Her overcoat was thick and red and bore a bright green Christmas ornament beside her left lapel. Beneath the coat she wore a red-and-white knit dress that fell to just below her knees, with red leather high-heeled boots that reached her hemline. She wore creamy white pearls at her neck and ears. Her lips were cranberry red, her eyes a misty blue. With her gloved hands, she gripped the ivory knob of an ebony walking cane and leaned heavily, her shoulders stooped with age.

The woman closed the door behind her then turned and looked around the room. "Well, I'll swan. Somebody's been busy."

"Hello." Amy stepped from the hallway.

"There you are," the woman said with a smile. "You must be Amy. Riley called so I wouldn't think you were a burglar. I'm Fanny. Fanny Lewiston, the bookkeeper."

"Hi, Fanny. I promise, I didn't touch anything on or in your desk."

"Oh, not to worry, dear. I wouldn't have

minded if you had. You were in the army with our Brenda, I hear."

"That's right."

They spoke for several minutes, with Fanny complimenting her office-cleaning job. Finally Amy had to take advantage of Fanny's presence and run out for lunch while someone was there to answer the phone.

"You go on and eat, dear. I'll man the fort."

Amy pulled on her coat, grabbed her bag from beneath her desk, and left. A cold, sharp wind nearly sucked the breath from her lungs. So much for the mild weather. And so much for walking to lunch. She drove five blocks to the pizza parlor. A half hour later she drove back to the office, chewing gum to get rid of her pepperoni breath.

Riley's truck sat next to the door. He was back. When she entered, the office felt considerably smaller than it had when she'd left. There was still plenty of room; the space wasn't that small. But she seemed to have some sort of internal radar that made her nerves twitch whenever she got within ten feet of Riley Sinclair.

Chapter Five

"You're back," Riley noted, sounding slightly surprised. "You weren't gone very long."

Amy hung up her coat and stuffed her bag under her desk. "Long enough to grab a slice of pizza. Did anything exciting happen while I was gone?" she asked them.

The elderly woman winked at her. "Riley came in. That's always exciting."

"Fanny," Riley drawled, "you keep up that sassy talk, you'll turn my head. Next thing I know, Albert will be calling me out for making time with his wife."

Fanny tittered like a young girl. "Oh, go on with you. You better watch this one," she told Amy. "He's a sweet talker, he is."

"I'll watch him. Did you get that problem taken care of this morning?" she asked him.

"Turned out to be a simple misunderstanding. Maryann thought we were forgetting her laundry room."

"You can't forget a lady's laundry room," Fanny stated.

"I wouldn't dream of it."

Amy mentioned the pile of paperwork that she had moved from the surface of her desk into the hanging files and asked what Riley wanted done with them.

"You filed them?" he asked, a pained look on his face.

"More or less. Should I not have?"

"Oh, no, you did fine. I guess I was just hoping you lost them or burned them so we wouldn't have to deal with them."

"And when the IRS decides to audit you..." Fanny finished with a *tsk, tsk, tsk.*

"Yes, Mother," Riley said.

Fanny let out a huge sigh and smiled. "Very well, then. My work here is done for the day." She rose and tottered with her cane and her high-heeled boots over toward her coat.

Amy reached it before she did and helped her into it.

"Thank you, dear. You're a sweet one, you are. I'll see the two of you tomorrow."

"Do you need a ride home?" Amy offered.

"Oh, no, dear, but thank you. I've got my car."

The only other car nearby was a huge ten-year-old Lincoln, parked at the curb in front of the grocery store next door. Sure enough, Amy discovered as she looked out the window, Fanny made a bee-line straight for the Lincoln.

Amy watched until Fanny started the car and pulled away from the curb, then returned to her desk shaking her head.

"She's something, isn't she?" Riley asked.

"I'll say. Does she always dress like that?"

Riley blinked. "Like how?"

"All dressy like that."

"I don't know."

"You don't…Never mind." Men could be so oblivious.

"I mean," he offered, "I guess so. Does it bother you?"

"Of course not. I don't care what anyone wears.

I was just curious. You don't expect me to dress fancy like that, do you? With pearls and skirts and high-heeled boots?"

He eyed her carefully, as if wondering if she might bite.

"What's wrong?" she asked. "What did I say?"

"Nothing. It's just that a man would have to be a fool if he didn't want to see you in high-heeled boots and a skirt. But I don't imagine we're talking about the same thing."

Amy arched her brow, her pulse suddenly racing. "No, I don't imagine we are. Let me rephrase my question. Is my current mode of dress acceptable for the office, or do I need to wear the girl version of a suit? Keeping in mind that if I have to wear a suit, so do you."

"Fair enough. You wear whatever you want. But I'm not wearing a suit."

While Amy would rather take a bullet than wear ruffles or lace, she sometimes toyed with the idea of learning how to dress a bit more stylishly but she kept that to herself. If she mentioned such an inane thing to Riley, he might think she was fishing for a compliment, or seeking assurance that she was fine the way she was.

Clothes. What a stupid thing to worry about.

She and Riley spent the next several minutes going over the things he expected of her regarding the job, and how he thought she might manage the various elements of the office.

"Of course, I've never had an office manager before, so I can't really say how it should work," he admitted. "I guess we'll just make it up as we go. As long as my business gets taken care of and I can find something reasonably fast when I need it, you've pretty much got a free hand. Except for Fanny. Fanny has a job here until she or I decide otherwise. She works a couple of afternoons a week and takes off most of December and whenever her great-grandchildren come for a visit."

"No problem, but I'll want to examine what she's been doing, how the records are kept. I assume you have an outside accountant prepare tax returns."

"Yes. Fanny gathers all the information for him and he takes it from there."

"What do you do about payroll and accounts payables when she takes off?"

"Watch the mail for bills, and write a few checks."

They went over a few more details, then he walked her through the attached warehouse. "The shop," he called it. Aside from a small office in the near front corner, and across from it what appeared to be a small storage or utility closet, the entire building was open from front to back, with no walls to break up the space.

Overhead, large round ducts wrapped in thick insulation crisscrossed the warehouse up in the rafters, leading to several giant vents that would blow hot air to heat the building when it was in use in winter. Right now it wasn't in use, so no heat. Which was more than obvious. Within a minute Amy was shivering.

"Cold?" Riley asked with concern. "I'm sorry. I should have made you get your coat." He placed an arm around her shoulder and pulled her to his side, rubbing his hand up and down her arm.

Startled by his sudden move, Amy turned slightly toward him and looked up. Finding herself so close, touching him all the length of her body, his face so close to hers as he looked down at her, she sucked in her breath. In the process, three things happened. First, their gazes, barely a hand's-breadth apart, locked with each other. Second, the side of her left breast pressed against his firm, warm chest, making both breasts swell, both nipples harden and point. Third, his scent, male and fresh and arousing, filled her lungs.

And none of that took into account that her lips were so close to his that she felt the warm tingling, as if he had already kissed her. As if she was waiting for him to kiss her again.

In the cold air of the shop, their breath came out in cloudy puffs. He parted his lips, and so did she. Yet neither moved, neither spoke, until finally, they spoke at once.

"We should—" he began

"I didn't—" she started.

"You go," he offered.

"No, you."

"I was just going to suggest—" He slipped his arm from her shoulders and stepped back a scant inch, just far enough so that they were no longer touching. "—that we get back to the office before you freeze."

Freeze? With the heat from his body so near? Not a chance, she thought. But he was right. They had no business snuggling up together, out here all alone with each other in this big, empty warehouse.

"You're right," she murmured.

Once back inside, she got herself a cup of coffee and returned to her desk.

"How often do you work out there?" she asked. Anything to put them back on even footing.

"Whenever we have to. We prefer to work directly on site. But sometimes that's not possible. That's when I sometimes let a crew use the shop. Sometimes I use it myself. But mostly it's a warehouse."

"Is there an inventory list somewhere?" she asked.

"Right here." He tapped a finger to his temple.

"You're kidding. That's it? In your head?"

"That's it."

She gave him a serious frown. "I'll be taking inventory in the days and weeks to come and we'll keep it on the computer. No offense to your memory."

He gave her a cheesy grin. "None taken."

If Amy thought she and Riley might be more comfortable with each other after that exchange, time proved her mistaken. Over the next days, she found herself going out of her way to avoid eye contact, and making sure she didn't put herself within touching range of him. She stepped over to look out the window or looked down to study the contents of a drawer more times than she cared to count.

By the time she realized what she was doing, she realized that he seemed to be pulling the same avoidance maneuvers. Of course, for her to realize he wouldn't meet her gaze, she had to look at him. If anyone was watching the two of them, they were probably getting a good laugh. There they were, two grown people, so uneasy with each other that they scarcely talked, never got near each other, wouldn't look at each other, used anyone handy— poor Fanny got it most often—as a go-between. And she looked suspiciously as if she was about to burst into laughter at any moment.

The thing was, Amy didn't feel like laughing in the least. The entire scenario frustrated and saddened her. Finally, she waited until Fanny left for the day, then decided to confront Riley.

She crossed the room into his territory and sat on the chair before his desk. "Do you have a minute?"

He took his time looking up from the set of plans he was going over before answering. "Sure. What do you need?"

She took a deep breath, then let it out. "Is this going to work? The two of us working together?"

He frowned. "What do you mean? Are you not happy here?"

"It's not that. It's this awkwardness between us."

He blinked. "What awkwardness?"

She all but snorted. "I know men are supposed to be thickheaded, but really, Riley. You know as well as I do how awkward we've both acted with each other ever since that day in the shop, when you—when we—"

"When we—?"

"Look. I know you didn't mean anything by it." Her mouth started running and she couldn't seem to stop it. "I mean, even if you have been alone since Brenda shipped out, you wouldn't have meant what nearly happened the other day in the shop, I know that. I mean, you're used to Brenda, and she was so beautiful, so totally feminine even in combat boots. I know I'm nothing like that, not feminine or sexy or anything."

It was a good thing he chose that instant to speak, because her mouth had just run dry, of words and of spit. That might have had something to do with the enormous heat that suddenly flooded her face.

"Of course you are," he blurted out. He stared at her, wide-eyed. He swallowed. He looked away. "I mean…it doesn't take…."

When he didn't continue, she said, "Doesn't take what?"

He shrugged and thumbed the corner of the plans on his desk. "A woman doesn't need ruffles and lace to attract a man."

Her stomach did a little flip-flop. "What are you talking about?"

"Why, Sergeant Amy." He looked as if he was finished with awkwardness. His lips were curving upward and his eyes twinkled. "Are you fishing for compliments?"

Amy sputtered. Then, seeing his grin widen, she narrowed her eyes. "Are you laughing at me?"

He leaned forward and placed his forearms on his desk. "I think I'm laughing at both of us. Tiptoeing around each other like the other one's got the plague."

"It's not that bad," she claimed, her own lips twitching now. "Cooties, maybe."

He coughed to disguise his laughter, but there was no denying it was there. "You sound like one of my girls."

For one brief instant, she wondered what it would be like to be Riley's girl. Not his daughter, his girl.

Your best friend's husband?

Good grief. Brenda was dead and gone, God love her. Her husband was fair game, wasn't he?

Oh, and didn't that sound trashy?

"Well, I'm not one of your girls, I'm your employee."

"And I'm your boss, which means that, if you count what I was thinking, I was way out of line out in the shop and I'm sorry. You won't have to worry about me hitting on you again at work."

At work? What did that mean, that he was going to hit on her away from work? "Fair enough."

"Good. Friends?" He stood, and they shook on it.

"Friends."

And really, she thought to herself, wasn't friends better for everyone?

Then why did she suddenly feel so depressed?

That night at home, Riley still couldn't get over the curious look Amy had given him when he'd sworn not to hit on her at work. He'd been a jerk to add "at work" to the promise. She was probably thinking she was going to have to keep watch over her shoulder when she left work, with a qualification like that.

He'd been trying to reassure her. He hadn't really hit on her in the first place, had he? But maybe, as a woman alone with a large man in an empty warehouse, maybe she'd been frightened.

Bull. With the training she got before shipping out to Iraq, she could probably beat the stuffing out of him. And that had not been fear in her eyes when they'd nearly kissed.

So maybe that look today, when he'd said "at work," had been relief that he hadn't shut the door completely?

He shook his head. Who knew the mind of a woman. He'd never truly known a woman other than Brenda. The thought of getting to know a new woman in that way had not appealed to him until Sergeant Amy came to town.

Was it too soon? Was it fair to Brenda?

He wasn't talking about marriage, but he wouldn't mind a date, spending time with a woman his own age. Maybe share a few kisses. Maybe sweat up the sheets now and then.

Could he do that? Could he have a casual, or even a serious, affair, while sharing a home with three curious little busybodies?

Only a crazy person would even think of such a thing.

Putting three little girls to bed an hour later didn't particularly help his sanity any, but he loved every minute of it. They kept him grounded, lifted his heart. They made him smile and laugh and cry and bang his head against the wall on nearly a daily basis. They filled him with terror for the future, and hope. And so much love, he couldn't contain it all.

Thank you, Brenda, for our girls. How am I supposed to raise them alone?

A moment later he was ready to swear he truly was going insane. He thought he heard Brenda's voice. The words were distinct, as if coming from right behind him. "Silly, you're not supposed to raise them alone."

He spun around, half expecting to see her standing there, laughing at him. "Silly." That's what she had always called him when she teased him.

She wasn't there, of course. No one was there.

It took a good thirty minutes for his heart rate to settle.

But when he slept that night, he dreamed of her. She came to him in his sleep and smiled. "I hope you like the present I sent you." Then she waved good-bye and left.

When he woke he realized he felt good. Cheerful. Usually when he dreamed of Brenda, he woke sad and lonely.

By the time he and the girls were ready to leave for the day, he remembered that he'd dreamed of Brenda, but couldn't remember what it had been about.

All he could do was put it aside and face the new day. To that end, when he got to work he decided that this close to Christmas, no one should have to be alone. Including his sergeant.

"What are you doing tomorrow morning?" he asked Amy.

"Uh, tomorrow's Saturday, right? My day off?"

"I'm not talking about work. The girls and I are picking out our Christmas tree tomorrow morning. Why don't you come with us?"

She stood there and stared at him, her eyes blinking, looking as if she might be calculating the national debt in her head.

He chuckled. "Was it that hard a question?"

"Oh. Sorry." She laughed at herself. "I was just trying to decide if I want a tree for my new apartment."

"You got an apartment? When? Where?"

"The Alameda Apartments, on Third. I move in this afternoon when I get off work."

"Congratulations. It's Friday, you've got a new apartment waiting for you. I expect you to take off at noon and call it a day."

"I'll take it," she said quickly.

"Do you have furniture to move?"

"No. The apartment's furnished. All I own is in my car and motel room. I travel light."

"Sounds like it. So how about the great Christmas tree hunt? It's not like we're going to the mountains to chop down a live tree. We're just going to that tree lot down the street."

"Darn. And me with my ax all sharp and ready. But I guess the lot down the street will do. While you get your tree, I'll get a small one for myself. I'll need a stand and decorations and lights. Is there someplace here in town to get them?"

"The hardware store has some, and so does the drug store. I think the feed store does, but unless you want to hang road apples on your tree—"

"Road apples?"

"Roundish, smelly items that horses leave in small piles on the road."

"What do they call them if they're not on a road?" she asked with an exaggerated wide-eyed look.

"Horse dung," he said straight-faced.

They both laughed. And it felt good.

Amy took Riley at his word and left work for the day at noon. She had checked out of her motel room that morning, so all she had to do was drive to her new apartment and unload her meager belongings. A few boxes of linens, kitchen items, personal items, a suitcase of clothes and not much else. The unloading took twenty minutes, but only because she took her time.

The Alameda Apartments was a grand name for a strip of six upstairs and six downstairs connected units, reddish-brown brick, with individual central heat and air. Each unit came with all the usual kitchen appliances, but no laundry facilities. Cable TV hookup came with the rent, but not a TV.

Amy's apartment was next to the south end, upstairs. The faint smell told her the walls had been painted recently, basic white. Brown carpet, worn in places, but still serviceable, covered the floor in the living room and bedroom. A throw rug or two would brighten up the place.

How about that? She'd had a decorating thought. Wonders never cease. Maybe there was hope for her yet. Decorating usually never crossed her mind.

Then, again, never before had she meant to settle in and put down roots, create a home for herself. Not that she intended to root in an apartment for the rest of her life, but it was a good place to start.

It was as nice as either of the two apartments she'd had before being deployed, and a hell of a lot better than any place she'd stayed in before moving out on her own. There had never been much room for her when she'd been juggled from relatives to foster care and back again from the time she was eight until her eighteenth birthday.

She hadn't complained during those years of sleeping on the floor, or on the sofa, or sharing a bed with some third girl cousin twice removed.

She'd known even then that things could have been a lot worse for her.

The first eight years of her life hadn't been much better than the years of shuffling around, but at least when she'd been younger, if she'd had to sleep in the car or a ratty motel, her mother had been with her.

But there would be no more of that rootless shifting from place to place for her. Tribute was it. She was sticking.

She spent the rest of the afternoon and evening unpacking, rearranging furniture, making the bed. And she made lists. The grocery list would be taken care of before the day was out. Other things such as a television, a new coffeemaker, maybe even a houseplant, would have to wait until she could make a trip to a larger discount store somewhere.

Maybe she would go to Waco tomorrow after the great Christmas-tree search.

Before the tree search, however, she got to show off her new apartment to Riley and the girls when they came to pick her up Saturday morning.

Her plan had been to watch for them, then run downstairs as soon as they pulled in, so they didn't have to wait for her. But a couple of minutes before they were due, she was drying her hands from a last-minute kitchen wipe-down when someone knocked on her door.

Her heart gave a little leap. *My first visitor.*

Of course, it had to be Riley, and she was right, partly. She opened the door to find Riley, Pammy, Jasmine, and Cindy.

"Surprise!" they shouted.

Amy laughed in delight and stepped back to let them enter. Her heart flip-flopped at the smile on Riley's face. "What's going on?"

"We come bearing gifts," Riley said.

"I brought this." Cindy held up a small flower-pot, decorated in Christmas red and green, with a miniature ivy trailing from it.

"How wonderful. Thank you." Amy was more touched than she'd been in a long, long time as she took the plant from those tiny hands.

"This one's from me." Pammy offered a pretty African violet in full, lilac bloom.

"Oh, Pammy, how gorgeous. Thank you."

"You can put them both on this," Jasmine said. From behind her back she pulled out a mirrored tray that would fit just right on her coffee table.

Amy thanked her profusely. She got all three girls to help her arrange and rearrange the tray and plants until they were all satisfied.

"I can't thank you girls enough," Amy said. "The whole apartment looks better now. I love my presents. Thank you." While the girls gave final approval of the presentation, Amy mouthed a silent *Thank you* to Riley.

"It was their idea," he claimed. "They thought it up and decided what they wanted to get you and picked them out themselves."

"I thank you for humoring them. I can't remember the last time I had a live plant, now I have two. Would you like the grand tour?"

"Naturally," he said.

What should have taken five minutes max, stretched into fifteen easily with the curiosity of three little girls to satisfy. The thing that seemed to fascinate them the most was living upstairs, with no back door, no yard, only one bedroom, and the tiny kitchen.

"But it's so small," Pammy protested.

"Not to me," Amy told her. "I'm the only person living here, so it's really just right."

That made the girl stop and think. "Oh. Okay."

Riley finally got his girls to stop asking questions and poking into cabinets long enough to get them out the door. He turned back and held out his hand for Amy.

"Come on. We have Christmas trees to buy."

Amy slipped her hand into his and felt a tingle race up her arm. She wanted to kiss him. But instead she closed the door behind them. "Yes. Christmas trees."

They smiled at each other and took the stairs side by side, hand in hand.

Chapter Six

The early-December Saturday morning was bright and sunny, cool and crisp, with a bit of a bite to the south wind. The Christmas-tree lot took up the outer quarter of the grocery-store parking lot. Several cars were parked nearby. A young couple walked hand-in-hand through the rows of trees, along with a family of four and an elderly couple.

As Riley pulled into a parking space he cautioned the girls, "Don't go wandering off. Stay together and stay with me."

The girls were busy staring out the window at

the Christmas trees, commenting on which ones they liked best.

"I'll take your promise on that," Riley added.

Still no response.

"Girls."

"Yes, Daddy," Jasmine said. "We'll stay together and stay with you. We promise. Don't we?" she added under her breath for her sisters.

"My little peacemaker," Riley murmured as he killed the engine.

They all piled from the truck and made their way to the tree lot. The salesman greeted them, then stepped back out of their way and let them wander.

Amy took in a deep breath. "Oh, it smells good here. It's been a long time since I smelled pine." The scent of the trees, the wind, the presence of the man who stirred her…it was all so heady.

"I'll bet," Riley said.

But there was no time to linger over the delightful scent. They had to hustle to keep up with the girls, flitting from one tree to another. They couldn't decide if they wanted the giant eight-footer or the cute twelve-inch predecorated tree in a foiled pot.

"I don't know what you're going to do about that monster," Amy told Riley, "but I see my tree right here." She picked up the small, decorated tree.

"Are you getting that one?" Pammy asked.

"I am. I think I'll set it in the middle of my new mirror tray, and put my other new plants on either side. How does that sound?"

"It sounds cool. Can we see it when you take it home?"

"Of course you can, as long as your dad says it's okay."

"Can we, Daddy?"

"I think we can work that into our schedule. But first we have to pick a tree. Preferably one that will fit in the house."

From that point on, Amy seemed to lose control of her day. She tried to hang back and let Riley and the girls choose their tree without her tagging along, but they would have none of it. Riley asked her opinion on every tree they considered. He had apparently made up his mind to include her in this family outing and that was that.

It was the sweetest time Amy remembered ever spending. The rush of cold wind, little-girl giggles, the ever-present zing of attraction with an attentive man. And all of it ordered up especially for her.

That, at least, was what it felt like.

The girls and Riley finally settled on a beautifully shaped pine to grace their home. He tied the tree down in the bed of his pickup, and, with Amy holding her little tree in her lap, headed back to her apartment.

"You have to let us come up and help you situate your tree," Riley reminded her as he parked at her building.

"Of course," she claimed with feigned seriousness. "I might need help moving it around."

From the backseat, three young voices giggled.

Upstairs in her apartment the girls made a grand production of placing the cute little Christmas tree in the center of Amy's new mirror tray.

"How gorgeous," she claimed. "The mirror makes it twice as pretty."

She watched as the girls made a big fuss, turning the tree this way and that, switching places between the ivy and the African violet. Should the ivy be on the right, or the left? Smiling over their dilemma, Amy happened to glance toward Riley and caught him watching her. The warm smile in his eyes seemed to melt her insides.

"Thank you for including me this morning," she said softly.

"Thank you for coming with us," he replied.

"But now, since we helped you put up your tree, I think you should come help us with ours."

For a wild instant, she wanted to say yes. But it wouldn't be right. "That's a family time, for you and your girls. You don't need an outsider there."

"You're not an outsider," he protested. "This is the season of giving and sharing. No one should be alone this time of year, and we want to share this day with you, don't we, girls?"

"Yes." Jasmine nodded emphatically.

"You have to come help us, 'cause we helped you," Pammy decided.

Cindy, rather than speak, slipped her hand into Amy's and smiled up at her.

Amy was a goner and she knew it. "Well, since you put it that way, how can I refuse?" *And why would I want to?*

In what seemed like the blink of an eye Amy found herself helping untangle strings of lights in the Sinclairs' living room. Riley had already used his saw to trim the bottom of the tree. He had put it in a stand he'd had sitting out and waiting at the ready. Once the tree stood steady in the stand, he filled the stand with water, and Pammy helped him drape a red-and-green skirt beneath the tree to hide the stand. They had moved furniture around so the tree could occupy the place of honor before the wide window overlooking the front porch.

"Okay," Amy said a few minutes later. "That's it for this one. Can someone plug this in for me, please?" She was sitting on the floor amid strings of lights, too far away from the wall to reach the outlet.

"I can," Pammy offered.

Amy shot a quick glance at Riley, working on his own string of lights. He saw the question in her eyes—are kids allowed to plug things in? What did she know about kids? But Riley gave a slight nod, so Amy relaxed.

"Great," she told Pammy. "Thanks."

Pammy pushed the plug into the outlet, but nothing happened.

Amy groaned and laughed. This was her third string, and she'd had to check every bulb in all of them to find the one bulb in each string that was burned out. "Here we go again. I thought they made them now that didn't make all the lights go out just because one bulb quit working."

"They do," Riley acknowledged. "Or so I'm told. These things are antiques."

"Nana and Gramps used to use them on their tree when Mama was a little girl," Jasmine explained. "Back in the old days."

Amy laughed. "The old days, huh?"

"Yeah," Riley said. "You know, right after Lee surrendered."

"Huh?" Jasmine said.

"Who's Lee?" Pammy asked.

"What's sumembered?" Cindy asked.

"Surrendered," Amy said automatically. "It means he gave up."

"Oh." Cindy wasn't particularly impressed. She was having too much fun playing with a bag of bows from packages of years past. Some of the bows still had enough adhesive on their backings to stick, evidenced by the red, green, and yellow bows stuck to the little girl's hair.

One by one, Amy checked each bulb until she found the one that required replacing, and the entire string lit up.

"Aha. Success."

"Me, too," Riley said as his string, too, lit up.

Finally they had all the light strings for the tree. Riley had a system—start at the top and wind around the tree, adding a new string when necessary, until the entire tree was covered.

Next came the decorations. Amy assigned herself the job of handing them out and left hanging them to Riley and the girls. Amy's heart constricted watching the girls brag about remembering this one and that one from last year.

Then she lifted out one of those decorations that contain a photograph. This one was of Riley, Brenda, and the girls. Cindy was a chubby little toddler. A lump rose in Amy's throat.

"What have you got there?" Riley asked.

She had to blink the moisture from her eyes before she could look up at Riley standing over her. "It's beautiful."

"Yes." He took the ball from her and held it gently in the palm of his hand. That was the dichotomy of the man, right there. Big, tough, calloused hands gently cupping a ball so delicate that he could crush it with a harsh look, but it was his family, precious and safe in his protection. The hard protecting the delicate, delicately. A strong man with a softness to capture a woman's heart.

"Is it us, Daddy?" Pammy asked, breaking the spell.

"It's us," he said softly.

"Lemme see," Cindy cried.

"Me, too." Jasmine stretched sideways to see around Cindy.

Riley knelt and held out the ornament so all his

girls could see. Then he stood. "Now, where should we put it?"

"Right here."

"No, up there."

"Over here."

"Okay," he said with a chuckle. "Now that we're all agreed, I'll just put it right here." He chose a spot halfway up, facing the room. He put it as near the outside of the limb as he could without endangering the ornament. "There. How is that?"

"Perfect," Amy whispered without thought.

"Yea!" the girls cheered.

Riley turned to Amy and held out his hand. "Okay, what's next?"

Amy looked away, then down into the box of ornaments. "Here." From her seat on the floor, she handed him the next one, and the next, and soon the ornaments from two large boxes adorned the evergreen.

"Is it time for the icicles yet?" Jasmine asked.

"Icicles!" Cindy cried.

"What about the garland?"

Chagrined that they'd nearly forgotten the garland, Riley did most of the work, starting at the top as with the lights, and letting the girls help drape it around the lower limbs.

"Now the icicles?" Cindy demanded.

"No," Riley said. "Not quite yet. Something else is missing." He arched his neck and peered up at the top of the tree. "I wonder what it could be."

"The angel," Jasmine said.

"Oh, the angel," Pammy agreed.

"Can I put her on?" Cindy asked.

"The three of you decide," he said. "I might be able to lift two of you up there, but not three."

"Amy can lift me," Cindy offered.

A little thrill raced through Amy.

Riley looked at her, his brow raised. "Would you mind?"

"Mind? I'd be honored."

It took some maneuvering to get everyone within reach. Amy lifted Cindy, and Riley hefted Pammy and Jasmine. Then they had to stop and start over because they'd forgotten the angel. She stood about eight inches tall and was dressed in a beautiful white lace gown, with miles of angel white hair, with a silver halo and wings.

Eventually all three girls had a hand on the angel and put her on the top of the tree.

"Wait," Jasmine complained. "She's crooked."

Amy could barely speak around the lump of emotion in her throat. She had never participated even remotely in putting the angel atop a Christmas tree. To have this family that was so important to her include her this way, in fact, need her help for this ritual, nearly undid her.

"Your daddy can straighten her," she managed.

Riley shot her a look of gratitude. He was getting tired hoisting two wiggling girls up in the air at once. He set the girls down and huffed and puffed as if he'd run ten miles. "You girls are getting too big to heft around like that."

"Aw, Daddy, we are not."

"Okay, maybe not. But by next year," he said.

When Amy set Cindy down, Riley reached up and straightened the angel.

Pammy grinned. Jasmine clapped.

"*Now* can we do the icicles?" Cindy demanded.

"Yes, Cindy, we can do the icicles now," Riley said. "Amy, the icicles, if you please."

"Certainly." She handed him a box of icicles. When he took it, their fingers brushed. It seemed as if his lingered on hers a little longer than necessary, a lot shorter than she wanted. When he took his hand away a shiver ran up her spine. A shiver of warmth.

Then they made her laugh with their debate over which method was best, the "one or two strands carefully arranged" method versus the "grab a handful and throw it on" method. Cindy loved to throw while the two older girls carefully draped theirs one strand at a time. Riley sided with Cindy, but spent most of his time doling them out to her a couple at a time so she wouldn't throw large clumps at the tree.

This is how a true family behaves, Amy thought, imprinting the picture permanently in her mind.

Oh, she wasn't naive enough to think that the Sinclairs were perfect or that they always got along so well or were always so happy and loving as they were this day. But the bonds were there and they were strong. Nothing was going to tear this family apart. Not even death, she thought. The death of their mother and wife. Even without Brenda, they were still bound, maybe tighter than ever.

And the love, she thought with quiet envy. It was there in their eyes. Love, laughter, respect for each other.

She knew the girls had no idea how lucky they were to have each other, to have this man as their father. To have had Brenda as their mother. Her voice and her face might fade from their minds in the years to come—or perhaps not, if they hung on to the Christmas presents Amy had brought them from Iraq—but their mother would always be in their hearts, and they would never forget the essence of her, her love for them. In that, they were blessed. And while Amy was truly glad for them, somewhere inside her was the little girl she'd once been, wondering why her mother didn't love her, why she kept getting shuffled from uncle to aunt to cousin to foster care.

She prayed that these darling girls never had to learn how lucky they were.

"Hey."

At the soft voice, Amy blinked and found Riley kneeling before her.

"What's wrong?"

Amy smiled. "Nothing. Absolutely nothing. Thank you for including me with your family today. You have no idea how special this has been for me."

He stroked one finger down her cheek. "You have no idea how glad I am that you're here."

His touch made gooseflesh rise on her arms. His words made butterflies flutter in her heart.

"Mistletoe, mistletoe!"

"Uh-oh." Riley pushed himself to his feet, then extended a hand for Amy. "Brace yourself," he warned as he pulled her to her feet. "They like to kiss."

"Well, that's convenient," she said before she could stop herself. "So do I."

His brow arched and his lips curved upward. "Glad to hear it."

Oh, yeah, she should have kept her mouth shut. He looked at her now as if she were the last morsel on the plate and he was starving.

She quickly moved away, toward the girls. Away from temptation.

"Amy, look at me."

Amy looked at Cindy as instructed. The child held a sprig of mistletoe over her own head and beamed up at her. Amy gave her an exaggerated frown. Folding her arms over her chest, she tapped one finger against her own lips.

"Do you know you've got leaves sticking out of the top of your head?"

Cindy giggled, then hiccuped. "It's not leaves, silly, it's mistletoe. You're supposed to kiss the person under the mistletoe. It's a costume."

"Custom," both her sisters corrected.

"Really? Well, if it's a custom…" Amy leaned down and kissed Cindy on the nose, making the girl giggle and hiccup again.

They took turns, with Cindy finishing up her turn by getting kisses from everyone else. Pammy

NO POSTAGE
NECESSARY
IF MAILED
IN THE
UNITED STATES

BUSINESS REPLY MAIL
FIRST-CLASS MAIL   PERMIT NO. 717-003   BUFFALO, NY

POSTAGE WILL BE PAID BY ADDRESSEE

SILHOUETTE READER SERVICE
3010 WALDEN AVE
PO BOX 1867
BUFFALO NY 14240-9952

Get FREE BOOKS and FREE GIFTS when you play the...

LAS VEGAS

GAME

Just scratch off the gold box with a coin. Then check below to see the gifts you get!

YES! I have scratched off the gold box. Please send me my **2 FREE BOOKS** and **2 FREE GIFTS for which I qualify.** I understand that I am under no obligation to purchase any books as explained on the back of this card.

335 SDL EF4S   235 SDL EF5U

FIRST NAME	LAST NAME

ADDRESS

APT.#	CITY

STATE/PROV.	ZIP/POSTAL CODE

(S-SE-12/06)

7	7	7	Worth TWO FREE BOOKS plus TWO BONUS Mystery Gifts!
🍒	🍒	🍒	Worth TWO FREE BOOKS!
🔔	🔔	♣	TRY AGAIN!

www.eHarlequin.com

Offer limited to one per household and not valid to current Silhouette Special Edition® subscribers. All orders subject to approval.

held the mistletoe over Jasmine's head, and they all took turns kissing her. Jasmine returned the favor, but had to stand on a footstool to do it.

Then it was Riley's turn, but he declared that not all the ladies had had their turn yet and held the sprig over Amy's head.

The girls cheered and took turns kissing her on the cheeks, the nose, and before Amy could make an excuse and duck away, Riley kissed her on the lips. A kiss so fast and light that there was no way anyone could take offense.

But the spark it ignited was potent. If the girls hadn't been there, Amy knew she and Riley would soon be rolling on the floor, their mouths fused, their hands seeking, and their clothes in a pile under the Christmas tree. By the look in his eyes, she wasn't the only one who knew it.

They had to do it all again when Riley hung the mistletoe above the doorway and the girls made him stand beneath it so they could all kiss him. Laughing and giggling, they pushed and shoved Amy into place. There was no help for it, she had to kiss him. For the girls.

Yeah, right. For the girls.

She brushed her lips against his cheek then stepped away.

Riley gripped her hand and held her close to his side. How was she supposed to regain her equilibrium with his thumb drawing little circles on the palm of her hand?

They all stood around the tree, admiring her handiwork.

"It's beautiful," Amy murmured.

"It'll be even prettier when it gets dark outside," Pammy said.

"Let's go see if we can see it from the porch in the daytime," Jasmine suggested.

The girls headed for the front door in a flash.

"Put your— Never mind," Riley said to the front door as it closed behind them. "I guess they won't freeze to death in the short time they'll be outside."

Then, without a word, he took her by the hand and rushed her around the corner and into the kitchen. He gripped her shoulders and looked down at her. His eyes were dark, his nostrils flared.

"If you don't want me to kiss you, push me away right now."

"You're wasting time." She slid her arms beneath his and pulled him close.

He swooped, his mouth taking hers before hers

could take his. He invaded her mouth and her senses, heating her blood, her skin. Stealing her breath. Softening her heart.

She drank him in. His taste was dark and minty. His scent, of pine and fresh air. She reveled in the kiss, in him. Never had she felt such completeness and never had a kiss made her yearn so strongly for more.

They might have kissed forever, or slid to the kitchen floor and made love right there, but for the sound of the front door opening and three little girls giggling.

Riley and Amy tore apart, chests heaving, eyes wide. She was gratified that his eyes looked as startled as she felt.

"Wow," he whispered.

She couldn't help but smile. "Yeah." Then she remembered who she was kissing, and her smile slipped away. Her heart sank. "Wow." It shouldn't have happened, that kiss. And it damn sure shouldn't have been a *wow*.

"Daddy? Amy?" Pammy called.

Riley huffed out a breath and stepped away from Amy. "We're in the kitchen," he called out. "Close the front door."

"Yes, sir."

Amy didn't think she could face the girls. She felt too shaky on the inside. She had to get out of there. She pushed past Riley and retrieved her coat and bag from where she'd left them in the dining room.

"What are you doing?"

Amy jumped as if she'd just been caught stealing the family silver. "You startled me."

"Glad to hear it." He leaned against the kitchen doorway and folded his arms across his chest. "I'm a little startled myself. Is that why you're running?"

"Running?" She shrugged into her coat. "I guess that's as good a word as any, but I prefer to think of it as a strategic retreat." She hefted her bag and whirled toward the hall door. And there stood three little girls.

"Are you going?" Pammy asked.

"You could stay longer, couldn't you?" Jasmine asked.

Cindy poked out her lower lip in a champion pout. "Don't go."

"Sorry kiddo." She smoothed a hand down Cindy's hair and smiled at the other two girls. "But it's time for me to go back to my apartment. I still have some shopping to do so I can live there."

"Okay, girls, get your coats back on. We'll take Amy home."

"No, that's okay," Amy said quickly. She edged her way around the girls, keeping as far away from Riley as possible while inching her way toward the front door. "It's only a few blocks, and the weather's great. I can walk."

"Don't be silly. I wouldn't dream of letting you walk home."

Ah, saved by the autocratic male. He'd just given her the perfect excuse to make her escape. She stiffened in feigned irritation. "Letting me? I beg your pardon. Nobody *lets* me do anything. I'm walking home because that's what I choose to do, thank you very much."

She almost made it out the door.

"Amy, are you mad at us?"

"Oh, sweetie, no." Amy dropped to her knees and held out her arms.

Little Cindy launched herself at Amy's chest. "I don't want you to go."

"Oh, Cindy, it'll be all right. We'll see each other again real soon. Thank you for my plant, and for helping me arrange my little tree, and for letting me help trim your tree."

Cindy heaved a melodramatic sigh, playing her distress to the hilt. "You're welcome."

Amy pulled away and waited until Cindy looked up at her. "Are we still friends?"

Cindy finally smiled. "Okay."

Amy didn't wait. She said good-bye to the two older girls, then, without looking him in the eye, to Riley. Never had she made such an awkward exit in her life.

Monday morning, little Cindy couldn't wait for her pre-kindergarten class to be over so she could go across the street to Nana's. She went to Nana's every day, but today was special. Today she was bursting to tell Nana all about the presents they took to Amy for her new apartment, and how they helped her arrange her tiny Christmas tree on the pretty tray they gave her, and how she came home with them and helped them decorate their big tree and lifted her in the air to help with the angel, and how they all kissed each other under the mistletoe. It was all so neat and wonderful to Cindy that she wanted to share it with her favorite adult. Well, favorite except for Daddy.

But Nana didn't act like she cared much. She just frowned and muttered under her breath a lot.

"What's the matter, Nana? Don't you feel good?" Cindy asked.

"I feel fine, honey. I'm just sorry I wasn't there to help you trim your Christmas tree."

"Me, too," Cindy said. "Then you and Grandpa could have kissed Amy under the mistletoe, too."

Chapter Seven

Amy was glad that Monday was so busy at the office. Neither she nor Riley had time to say more than ten words to each other, and those were all business.

Tuesday proved more of the same, until four o'clock when Marva and the girls descended on the office with boxes and bags in tow.

Amy was delighted to see the girls, and they her.

As for Marva, this was only the second time Amy had seen her. She wasn't expecting warm hugs, and it was just as well, because she barely got a civil nod as Marva passed her desk and headed in to see Riley.

There being no such thing as privacy in the office, outside of the restroom or the storage closet, Amy couldn't help but overhear when Marva explained the reason for their visit.

"I hear you finally put up your Christmas tree at home," the woman said to Riley.

"Yes. We did it Saturday. You'll have to come by and see it."

"Yes, well, I drove by this place and noticed you haven't done anything here, at least nothing that's visible from the street. So we've come to remedy that, haven't we, girls?"

"We're gonna decorate," Jasmine said firmly.

"There's not enough room for a tree," Riley cautioned.

"I do have some sense," Marva stated. "Just some window dressing and the like. You just go on about your business and I'll take care of everything. You can count on me."

"I know I can." He smiled quickly.

Amy was then witness to the slickest bit of military command she'd seen in a while. Marva Green might resent the military for controlling most of her life via her husband and sons and for taking her daughter from her, but that hadn't kept her from absorbing command technique. She had all three girls, and, eventually, Riley, too, marching to her tune and carrying out her orders in nothing flat. In under thirty minutes a beautiful garland and tinsel with blinking lights draped the front window and produced a pretty holiday picture from the sidewalk and street.

Not that Amy was invited to the viewing with the family, but she heard the reviews and knew what it looked like from inside.

On the office door Marva had Riley hang a wreath that was so large he had to turn sideways to enter, or risk knocking the wreath off with his shoulder.

Not willing to let well enough alone, Marva draped garland around the hallway door, and placed a red candle on top of a file cabinet in Riley's area.

Riley decided to keep the girls with him at the office, as he planned to go home shortly anyway.

Marva seemed disappointed not to take the girls with her, but she was nothing if not dignified as she put on her coat and moved toward the door.

"The decorations are beautiful, Mrs. Green," Amy offered.

Marva paused with one hand on the doorknob. "Why, thank you, my dear." She tilted her head and studied Amy a moment. "Do you mind if I ask you a question?"

"Of course not," Amy said.

"Do you dress like that every day?"

Amy frowned and looked down at her white shirt and blue jeans. "Pretty much. What's wrong with it?"

Marva gave a delicate sniff. "Nothing, if you're a man."

Amy's back stiffened. "What are you, the fashion police?"

From the other end of the room came a masculine choking sound, accompanied by little-girl laughter and giggles.

"Well!" Marva claimed in a huff. "I never."

"Of course you never," Amy said. "I forgot, you're not the fashion police, you're the dragon lady."

Pain flashed through Marva's eyes. She turned quickly and let herself out the door.

"Me and my big mouth," Amy muttered. She dashed out the door after the woman. "Mrs. Green, wait, please."

With her car door open, the woman stood and waited.

"I'm sorry. That was Brenda's nickname for you, I know. And you have to know that she said it with love. It was her way of acknowledging the differences between the two of you. She loved that you cared enough about her to want her to look her best all the time, even though she didn't always agree what that meant. But I shouldn't have called you that anyway. I'm sorry. It was her name for you and I have no right to it."

Waves of fury seemed to radiate from the ashen-faced woman. "That's right, you have no right to it. And that's her family in there, and you have no right to them, either. Or is that the reason you want them? Because they were Brenda's?"

Wow. A sucker punch. Amy hadn't expected that one.

Neither had Riley. She hadn't heard him follow her outside, but she heard him now as he sucked in a sharp breath in shock.

Marva was shocked, too, when she realized that Riley had overheard her remark. With her face flaming red in embarrassment, or perhaps renewed anger, she slid into her car and drove away.

Riley told himself he wasn't a coward, but he knew he lied. He should have talked to Amy right then and there when Marva threw out that bomb about Amy having no right to him or the girls, because they were Brenda's.

She'd accused Amy of only wanting what was Brenda's because they were Brenda's.

That was nonsense. He didn't believe it for a second. But the stricken look on Amy's face concerned him. Did *she* believe it? Did she fear she was attempting to take over her best friend's life?

He didn't have a clue what to say to her, or if he should say anything at all. So he did the only sane and sensible thing. The manly thing. The super-duper macho thing. He grabbed the girls and ran.

And the next day he did an admirable job of avoiding her by staying out on one site or the other most of the time.

Amy nearly snarled in frustration. Fanny was gone on vacation until after New Year's so Amy was fighting her way through payroll. Then there was the paperwork requiring Riley's signature, which wasn't ready until after he had disappeared back out to the site. Or wherever. He'd said he wouldn't be back for the day.

Well, she wasn't going to put this off until tomorrow when he came back to the office. He'd said it was important. If she could get it to the express drop box at the post office by six it would still go out tonight.

If Mohammed wouldn't come to the mountain...

She closed the office at five, as usual, and drove to his house, gratified to find his pickup in the driveway.

"Avoid me now, boss man," she muttered.

Not that she'd been at all anxious to spend any time with him since Marva's crack the day before, because...because... Because just maybe Marva had seen into her heart and understood what was there better than Amy did herself. How was she supposed to talk with a man whose mother-in-law had warned her away?

No matter, Amy decided. She could easily drive herself crazy trying to make sense of her own motives, her own emotions. And wasn't that pathetic? How was she supposed to determine Riley's feelings if she didn't know her own?

But it wasn't his feelings she was after when she pulled into his driveway just after five. Only his signature.

She knocked on the door and waited, a pen in one hand and the papers, turned to the signature page, in the other. But it was Pammy who answered the door.

"Amy." The girl beamed at her. "Come in."

"Thanks, Pammy. I have some papers your daddy needs to sign."

"He's in the kitchen. Daddy! Amy's here!"

Unwilling to wait for him to come to her, Amy quickly made her way to the kitchen.

"Hey," he said, his hands occupied dicing potatoes. "What's up?"

"I need you to sign these so I can ship them out tonight."

"Oh. Okay, just a sec." He finished the potato he was chopping, then washed and dried his hands before turning toward her. He signed the papers and thanked her.

Feeling dismissed, she turned to go, but at the doorway, her frustration shifted from matters of work to personal matters. She stopped and pivoted. "Riley, I—"

"Amy, about—"

"Sorry," they said in unison.

"Go ahead," she said.

"Ladies first."

"Okay." She took a deep breath for courage, thinking she might rather march ten miles with sand in her socks than initiate this conversation, but she'd started it.

"About what Mrs. Green said. About you and the girls belonging to Brenda, that I have no right to you."

"You know that's just her pain talking," he offered.

"Partly," she agreed with a nod. "And part of it is jealousy."

"What?"

"I'm a woman invading her territory. Or so she thinks. To her, any woman represents a threat. If you have a woman in your life, you might not need her so much. The girls might not need her so much."

Riley moved to the kitchen table and sat down heavily. He looked a little thunderstruck, staring off into space. "I never thought of it that way, but yeah, it makes sense."

"Anyway, I thought we should talk about what she said, you know, that—"

"She said you have no right to me and my girls," Riley said. "Yes, we belonged to Brenda. We loved her, we'll always love her. We love Marva, too, even when she's a pain in the ass. She's saved our bacon dozens of times. When we need her, she's always there for us. But she doesn't have a say in my private life."

"I know that."

"Then what's the problem?"

"The problem is me," she admitted. "I'm the one who wonders if…"

He rose and crossed to her. "If what?"

"What if she's right? What if I heard so much about you and the girls and this town from Brenda that I associate with you because of that? Maybe somewhere inside I feel guilty because I lived and Brenda didn't, and now I'm trying to live the life she would have had. Her town, her husband, her children."

Riley scoffed. "That's ridiculous."

"What if it's not?"

"Well, then, maybe we're a good pair."

"How's that?" she asked.

"What if I'm only looking for someone to step in and fill Brenda's shoes? A replacement for the wife I lost, the mother my girls lost."

Amy smiled sadly. "A new bedmate, cook and nanny? That thought has crossed my mind a time or two. Not that I think you've got those kinds of feelings for me. I just...I don't know. I guess I don't trust my own mind where you're concerned, and maybe I don't trust yours, either, and I know none of it matters. I just don't want what Marva said to come between us and make us uncomfortable with each other. We're just friends. I know you're not interested in me that way."

"Oh, really? Says who?"

If lightning had struck her she wouldn't have been more shocked. "You don't mean that."

"You know I do. Are you going to tell me the interest isn't mutual?"

Amy swallowed. She wanted to lie, but those deep-blue eyes wouldn't let her. "No, but so what? What if we act on that interest? What if we make a go of it? What's to stop us from ending up hating each other when I realize you and the girls will always be Brenda's, and when you realize I will never be Brenda?"

One corner of his mouth quirked upward. "With that kind of thinking, we might as well say good-bye right now."

"You're laughing at me."

He nodded once, with a slight smile. "Some, yeah."

"I guess I had it coming."

"I guess you did." He took a step closer. "I propose a test."

She eyed him carefully. "What kind of test?"

"Have you finished your Christmas shopping?"

"What's that got to do with anything?"

"Humor me. It's an easy, yes-or-no question. Have you finished your Christmas shopping?"

Amy heaved a sigh. "All right, I'll play. No.

I need one last element for the girls' presents from Brenda."

"Can you tell me what this last item is? Where you might need to go to get it?"

"I want to get a backpack for each of them, to hold all the parts of their presents."

He tilted his head in curiosity. "You're really making me wonder what Brenda was up to. What you're up to."

"My lips are sealed."

"How about this. You and I drive over to Waco Saturday afternoon. I'll get a sitter for the girls, and we'll have dinner, maybe catch a movie if you want. Make a date out of it. See if we end up hating each other."

Amy smirked. "You know I didn't mean it would happen in one day."

"So humor me. We'll have a test date, see what happens."

She was tempted. More than tempted. "It's not smart."

"Then let's be stupid. Come on. What do you say?"

She could play coy and tell him she'd have to let him know. She could fool herself into thinking that if she postponed her answer she might get smart and turn him down. But she'd never been coy in her life, and now it seemed she wasn't even smart.

She nodded. "All right. Saturday afternoon. A test. To see how it goes. Great. No pressure there, right?"

He smiled. "Right."

She spun on her heel and made for the door. "I've got to get this package shipped."

Only on her way out the door did it occur to Amy that she could have said no.

Friday morning Riley was out of the office. Amy had little work to occupy her. She spent most of her time pacing the floor, hearing that mocking voice over and over in her mind—*Do you dress like that every day?*

This crazy outing tomorrow was supposed to be a test date. To see…whatever.

How long had it been since she'd been on a date? A genuine, honest-to-goodness, civilian date? She couldn't remember, but she was pretty sure there'd been a different president in the White House at the time.

What had she worn on that long-ago date? For that matter, who had she gone out with?

Never mind. The who wasn't important. What mattered was what she'd worn.

No, what mattered was what she was going to wear tomorrow, when the only thing she really knew how to wear was desert camouflage. Or Levi's. She was pretty good with Levi's.

Do you dress like that every day?

Yes, dammit, she did. But tomorrow she wanted something else. She only wished she knew what that was. However, she knew where to go to find out.

It was nearly noon. She locked up the office and drove in the direction she knew the elementary school to be. It wasn't hard to find. It was the place with all the little morning kindergarten and pre-kindergarten kids streaming out the door to the buses and cars waiting to take them home. She looked at the driveways across the street from the school for the big sedan she'd seen Mrs. Green drive, but all the driveways were vacant.

It stood to reason that the Greens would keep a nice car like that in the garage, especially during cold weather, although it was in the upper forties today and sunny. But as it turned out, she didn't need the appearance of the car to find the Green's house, all she needed to do was follow Cindy as she zipped up the neatest yard to the front porch where Marva Green stood with open arms and a smile.

"Brenda," she whispered. "Your babies are in good hands. Your mother loves them so much."

When the street cleared, Amy rolled forward and pulled into the Greens' driveway. By then Cindy and her nana had gone inside. Amy rang the doorbell and took a deep breath for courage. She'd faced armed insurgents with little concern. They were nothing, however, compared to the dragon lady.

The door opened and for once, Marva Green was at a loss.

"I apologize for showing up like this without calling first," Amy began. "But I had a feeling you might have hung up on me rather than invite me over."

Having gathered her wits, the woman assumed her queen-to-peasant look. "I assume you're going to tell me why you would want to be invited."

Amy took another deep breath. "I need your help."

"I beg your pardon?"

"I'm not your daughter. I loved Brenda. She was the sister I never had but always wanted. But I don't want to be her, don't want to take her place even if I could, which I couldn't. I want my own place, Mrs. Green. If that place is in Riley's life, well, that remains to be seen. He asked me to spend tomorrow afternoon and evening with him to finish Christmas shopping. I said yes because I'd like to spend some time with him away from work, to see how we get along."

"And you're telling me this why?"

"I'm rambling, I know. I do that when I get nervous, and you make me nervous."

Mrs. Green's lips twitched. "I'm sure."

"Yes, well, I'd rather face a spitting camel than Brenda's beautiful, perfect mother, but I don't know where else to turn."

"Please." Marva rolled her eyes. "The suspense is killing me."

"I want to dress a little more—stylish, I guess—tomorrow and I don't know how and no one is better at that than—"

Mrs. Green's brow quirked upward.

"—Brenda's mother," Amy finished.

Suddenly the woman frowned and peered at Amy. "Am I to understand that you're asking me to help clothe you for your date with Riley?"

"In a nutshell, yes." Then it was Amy's turn to frown. "Where's Cindy?"

"Here I am," the child said, running in from the hall. "Hi, Amy."

"Hi, Esmeralda. How ya doin'?"

Cindy giggled, then hiccuped, looking adorable in a red dress with ruffles at the hem, sleeves and neck. She looked as though she'd just walked out of a Christmas pageant.

"Who," Mrs. Green said, "is Esmeralda?"

"That's me, Nana. I'm Esmeralda." Cindy beamed with pride.

Amy's heart warmed. "It's my nickname for her," she told Mrs. Green.

"How come you're here?" Cindy asked Amy.

"I came to ask your nana to help me dress a little nicer." At Cindy's look of confusion, Amy added, "More like you, in a dress, than in jeans, like me."

"You mean, like a girl?" Cindy asked, all sweetness and innocence.

"Yes, like a girl."

"Are you gonna help her, Nana? Can I help, too?"

Marva Green smoothed a hand over the head of her youngest granddaughter, treasuring the silky softness of Cindy's beautiful hair, while eyeing this friend of Brenda's. Inside, grief and rage and love threatened to tear Marva apart, but she kept her expression as blank as possible.

How dare this interloper come to town and try

to insinuate herself into Brenda's place? How dare this Amy person be alive when Brenda was not? The nerve of the girl, expecting Marva to help her snare Riley. That's essentially what this amounted to, Marva knew.

Brenda, Brenda, what am I supposed to do? She wanted to throw Amy out on her head, yet the girl was a link to Brenda unlike any other link Marva had. And Brenda had loved this girl like a sister. Her phone calls and letters and e-mails had been full of Amy this and Amy that. To turn the girl away now would be a slap in Brenda's face.

In addition, Marva knew she couldn't hope that Riley would stay single and depend solely on her for help with the girls forever. This was the first time he had shown any interest in a woman other than Brenda. She could have hoped any new woman in his life would be someone local, someone she knew.

But Marva couldn't think of any local girl with the strength of character to fill Brenda's shoes, attract—and hold—Riley's affection, love the girls and stand up to Marva herself. Apparently it took an outsider. But this outsider knew a side of Brenda that no one else knew.

Marva wasn't certain she wanted to know any more of that side of her daughter.

Whatever, this woman was here and seeking her expertise. Marva knew she had no real choice but to help her. It would cost her nothing but a little time. To turn her down could prove the first step in the possible future loss of free and constant access to her granddaughters.

Marva swallowed her emotions. It took courage for Amy to come here and ask for help. She herself could demonstrate no less.

She looked Amy up and down. "How much time do we have?"

"No ruffles," Amy stated flatly as the big sedan parked in front of a boutique on Main Street.

"If you want my help, you'll have to listen to my advice."

"I know that, Mrs. Green."

"If we're going to do this, you might as well call me Marva."

The giant knot behind Amy's breastbone eased. The woman's offer was a huge milestone. Reaching it didn't mean everything was going to be sweetness and light—Marva had yet to decide to like her—but it might get them through the lunch hour.

"And no lace or bows," she added.

Marva smiled slightly and took on the tone of a mother putting off saying no to avoid an argument. "We'll see."

That, Amy thought with a cringe, did not bode well for her.

Marva was on a first-name basis with Darnelle of Darnelle's Boutique. The two of them spoke a language that was foreign to Amy. They took ordinary words and changed their meanings, words like trim and cut and bias.

"I think something that flows with her movements, don't you?" Marva suggested to Darnelle.

Darnelle's eyes lit. With dollar signs, undoubtedly. "I've got just the thing. Black jersey pants, wide legs, slightly flared."

"Oh, yes. Amy, what size are you, a six?"

Amy blinked. "Uh…"

"Oh, for heaven's sake." Marva *tsk*ed in irritation. "Let's find her a six and an eight. Although she is a tad on the lean side. Do you have them in a four?"

The six met with Marva's approval, but the slacks left Amy feeling practically naked. Though she did like the way they swayed with her movements. And they were soft on her bare legs.

Marva found a soft, thin sweater in a black-and-white swirl pattern that fitted her like a second skin.

"Are you kidding?" Amy protested. "I look practically naked."

"Don't be ridiculous," Marva stated.

"You look pretty, Amy," Cindy said.

Amy wondered what it said about her that she trusted the fashion advice of a four-year-old.

Chapter Eight

Early Saturday afternoon Amy paced her small living room and tried to calm her racing heart.

Any minute Riley was going to pick her up for the first date she'd had in years. Unless she counted going to the canteen on base in Iraq, which she didn't.

One more look in the mirror.

She kept wondering who that person was who stared back at her.

Marva hadn't stopped with the flowing pants and cashmere sweater on the lunch hour. Oh, no, not the dragon lady of Tribute, Texas. The local shops had all closed by the time Amy got off work Friday, but that didn't deter Marva, not when she had an entire Saturday morning to work with.

There'd been accessories: earrings—thank heaven Amy's ears were already pierced or Marva might have done the deed herself, with her teeth if necessary—a necklace to complement the bold design and delicate texture of the sweater, a long, narrow scarf to drape around her neck.

Then there were shoes. They selected plain black leather pumps with two-inch heels, but only because, it being December and cold, Amy refused to have her bare toes sticking out of the sandals Marva preferred. Amy was under strict orders, however, to purchase a nice pair of dressy high-heeled boots in Waco.

For a woman who hated the army, Marva Green sure could bark out orders like the most seasoned of drill sergeants.

Looking at herself in the mirror, Amy remembered the traumatic experience earlier that morning at the hair salon. Call her crazy, but when a stranger came at her with a pair of scissors and a gleam in her eye, Amy got nervous and started wishing for her M-16.

Who knew that a little snip here, another there, would transform her hair from a mess to tie back out of her way into this cute fluff that feathered around her head and, along with a judicious application of cosmetics, made her eyes look huge, her face delicate.

She let out a sigh. She was buying into the media's and society's hype of their definition of beauty. Shame on her. But she really liked what she saw in the mirror. She might not want to look like this every day—she certainly wouldn't want to go to all this trouble!—but for special occasions, or when she just felt like it, this was a look she liked.

A heavy knock on her door startled her.

Caught preening in the mirror like a teenager primping for her first date, with the prerequisite case of nerves to go with the affair!

No. Don't think *affair*. If she thought about where this date might lead, she'd never make it through the day.

With a quick spritz from the misty fragrance Marva had insisted she needed, Amy breathed slowly and opened the door to her date.

"Wow," he said, giving her a slow once-over that made her feel as if he was stroking her from head to toe. "You look great."

Once she got her breath back, Amy swallowed to keep a rein on the nervous giggle trying to break loose. "Not bad, yourself," she managed. He looked taller. Must be the cowboy boots, when he usually wore work boots. Or maybe it was the crisp, pressed denims that made his legs look a mile long. He wore a pale-blue shirt that made his blue eyes seem a deeper blue than ever. He wore the shirt tucked in, with a silver oval belt buckle etched with a rodeo cowboy riding a bucking bronc.

Top that with a tan suede Western-style jacket that made his shoulders look wider than usual, and she swore her heart went aflutter. Her heart had never gone aflutter in her life.

"Are you ready?" he asked.

Oh, yeah. "Um, let me get my coat." Marva would cringe if she saw this old parka with her nice clothes, but Amy wasn't about to freeze just to look good.

Then again… "How cold is it?" she asked.

"The most you'll need is a jacket, if you've got something lighter than the parka."

She did. It wasn't suede, like his, but it wouldn't make her look like Nanook of the North, either.

"All right, then, I'm ready." A date. *Gulp.*

* * *

The fifty-minute drive to Waco down the smooth, two-lane blacktop that led through farmland and pastures went by fast.

Amy had expected to feel as awkward as ever, as nervous as she'd felt at her apartment, but all of that faded away when she asked him about the girls and he told her of their latest escapades.

"And we were just about going to be on time, when Cindy comes to me with her hairbrush and says the brush is broken and doesn't work anymore."

"It doesn't work?"

"That's what she said. You gotta love the way a child's mind works. Her hair was so tangled that she couldn't get the brush through it, which meant it was broken. She wouldn't let her sisters help her, so I had to do it. You never saw such snarls. I asked her how her hair got so tangled up, and she came out with the most elaborate story about gremlins sneaking into their room at night and picking her hair up two strands at a time and tying them in knots."

Amy laughed at the imagination it took to come up with a story like that.

"All over her head until it was all snarled." He was

quiet for a minute. "You know what?" He suddenly tilted his head and shot her a curious glance.

"What?" she asked.

"It's nice to be able to talk about them to another adult besides their grandparents. My usual companions on the rare occasions when I go out are roofers or plumbers or guys I went to school with. Guys don't talk to each other about their little girl's tangled hair."

"No," she said. "I don't imagine they do. Not good for the macho image."

"How shallow does that make me?"

"It doesn't make you shallow, it makes you a normal man."

The conversation lulled while he passed a slow-moving hay truck. Then he chuckled. "Cindy came up with another good one this morning. She's evidently decided you're an important person in her life."

A little warm spot bloomed in Amy's chest. "Is that okay with you?"

Startled, he glanced at her before focusing again on the road. "Why wouldn't it be?"

"I'm an outsider."

"You are not," he protested quietly but firmly. "She puts you in the same category as her nana."

Amy swallowed. "As honored as I am, being in the same anything with Marva Green is downright scary."

Riley laughed. "That's what makes Cindy's latest story so funny. She's got it in her head that you and Marva went shopping together."

Amy pursed her lips and tried for a look of innocence.

"You didn't," he said. "You did? Did you?"

"Please. It's embarrassing."

"Ha! You're embarrassed that you went shopping with the dragon lady?"

"Not that," she corrected. "It's embarrassing that at my age I had to have help finding something to wear on a date."

"After what she said to you the other day at the office, you asked her to help you?"

"I did." He looked stunned. She laughed. "Don't worry about it. It's a girl thing. Now she knows I'm not a threat to her."

"Ah. So that's what that was about."

"Apparently. Anyway, Cindy didn't make it up. She's the one who got Marva to agree to help me, and she went with us yesterday on my lunch hour."

"I'm sure she was a big help," he said with a wry smile.

"Let's just say one of the gifts I have to find today is for Darnelle."

"Darnelle Hatch?"

"Let me guess—you went to school with her."

"Sure, but she was Darnelle Koch back then. Married Teddy Hatch."

"Whom you also went to school with."

He gave her a cheesy grin. "Of course."

"What's that like?" she asked, a soft yearning filling her. "Living among people you've known all your life, knowing that you can walk down any street in town and come across someone who is your friend."

"When you put it that way, it sounds perfect, but its got its ups and downs. On the down side, there is nowhere I can go in town without seeing someone I know."

"In other words, it's a two-edged sword?"

"You got it. There is no such thing as privacy. Everyone in town knows everyone else's business."

"I'm learning that," she said. "Ernie the mailman says Jack over at the hardware store drank too much and wrecked his daddy's car last week."

"Yup. And he had Ernie's cousin's daughter

with him. Which explains why Ernie's telling everyone in town. Jack's lucky that Ernie doesn't have a shotgun."

"Considering what Marva thought of me this time last week, I'm pretty glad she doesn't, either."

"So," he asked a moment later. "This isn't what Marva helped you pick out, is it?"

"Yes, it is. I know nothing about style or fashion. She and Darnelle basically had their way with me," she added with a slight shudder.

Riley laughed at her. "Maybe Marva's getting smarter with the years. I would have thought she'd go for ruffles and bows and lace."

"She might have, but I reminded her I'm a crack shot with an M-16, and I know where she lives."

Riley laughed, then shook his head. "I wish Cindy had something like that she could hold over Marva's head, and that she'd use it."

"Cindy? Why?"

"I'm afraid she's not forceful enough to tell anyone if she doesn't like the ruffles and bows her Nana gets her."

"Oh, no," Amy protested. "Those must be Cindy's idea."

"What do you mean?" He shot her a quick glance.

"While we were shopping I saw Marva try to interest Cindy in clothes that were more tailored, less frilly. Cindy didn't want any part of them. She kept going back to the real girly stuff."

"So much for me thinking the kid wasn't forceful enough to express her opinion. I wonder what else I don't know about my own children."

"Don't feel bad, Daddy. No parent ever knows everything about their kids. Remember back to your own childhood."

He rolled his eyes. "I'd rather not."

At the discount store in Waco, Riley helped Amy find backpacks. Each girl would get a pack sporting her own favorite cartoon character.

Amy helped Riley choose toys. He wanted to get them each a doll, but Amy said he also had to get each one something that didn't scream "stay home and have babies" to them.

"Not that there's anything wrong with staying home and having babies," Amy said quickly. "It's an admirable thing to do. It's a biological imperative. But girls need to know there are other choices."

"Of course they have other choices."

"Then offer them some."

"Like what?"

"I don't know. A chemistry set. Jigsaw puzzles. Paint-by-numbers."

Riley shot her a narrowed look. "You want me to turn three kids loose in my house with chemicals and paints and hundreds of little pieces of cardboard?"

Amy grinned and patted him on the cheek, ignoring the way her fingers wanted to linger. "Now you're getting the idea."

Before she could pull her hand away, he grabbed it and held it with his on the handle of their shopping cart. "In that case, I might have to insist that you be around to help me clean up the mess."

She smirked, thinking she had him now. "Is that an invitation?"

His thumb stroked her palm and made her shiver. His eyes stayed fixed on hers and stopped her breath.

"And if it is?" His voice, deep and soft, nearly melted her bones right there where she stood, between the toy trucks and the fishing lures.

"I'm...uh...oh, look." She grabbed the closest thing at hand. "A little toy construction set. Maybe one of the girls will want to go into the family business."

Without taking his eyes from her, he took the package and tossed it into the shopping basket.

Slowly he smiled. "If I didn't know better, I'd say I make you nervous."

"It's a good thing you know better."

"Uh-huh."

Amy needed a breather from the whirlwind spinning in her head. The whirlwind named Riley. She freed her hand from his hold and ran her fingers through her newly trimmed hair.

After paying for their purchases, they flipped a coin and decided on dinner first, then a movie.

For the next two hours they sat across from each other in a dimly lit steakhouse and talked. No teasing or innuendos this time, but true conversation. They talked more about the girls, about work and his dreams for his business, about Marva and Frank and their two sons. And they talked about Brenda.

Riley had a need to know more about Brenda's life in Iraq, and Amy had a need to talk about the friend who had died protecting her and others.

After the waiter brought their dessert, Riley shook his head in chagrin. "If this is our test date, I think I'm failing."

Surprised, Amy nearly fumbled her fork. "Why do you say that? I thought we were doing fine."

"Yeah, but when a guy is trying to worm his way into a woman's affections or seduce her into bed, he should probably think of something else to talk about besides his late wife. That's not exactly sweet nothings."

Amy chuckled. "Relax. For anybody else, you might be right. For you and me, *not* talking about her would be awkward."

He looked at her for a moment, then smiled. "You're right, aren't you?"

"Of course. But just so I'll know, which were you going for? My affections or my bed?"

She would wonder later if she'd done it on purpose, brought the sexual tension to a sharp peak in an instant.

Why else would she have asked such a question? "Both."

Was she out of her mind? Obviously, or she wouldn't have opened— *Both?* "Oh."

Riley laughed. "You've got that deer-in-the-headlights look. I love it."

"I'm not a deer, thank you very much. You're a sadist, enjoying watching someone flop around like a fish out of water."

"Oh, sorry, wrong metaphor?"

"Simile, actually."

"The fact that you know that is scary," he said.

"I have a feeling," she said, meeting and holding

his gaze, "that before this night is over, I might just scare myself."

His eyes slid almost shut. "If I hadn't promised you a movie…"

"What would you do?"

"Are you trying to drive me crazy on purpose?"

"The truth?" she offered candidly.

"Please. I feel like I'm dangling in the wind, here."

"Well, if you are, you're not dangling alone, because I'm right out there with you. I don't think I know what I'm doing. What we're doing."

One side of his mouth curved up. "At least you said *we*. Does that mean you see us together?"

Her heart rate kicked into high speed. She stared, dry-mouthed, at the swirl of raspberry sauce trailing across her cheesecake. Okay, he wouldn't be asking if he didn't want her to say yes, would he? If he didn't want there to be a *we*, he would change the subject. "I shouldn't."

"Why?"

"Because we barely know each other," she offered. "Because I don't think either one of us is sure about what we do or don't see in each other."

He reached across the table and covered her hand with his. "I don't have a crystal ball, and I don't want one."

"You don't want to see how everything will turn out?"

"No." He shook his head emphatically. "What if I'd foreseen what happened to Brenda? Maybe I would have decided not to marry her so I wouldn't have to lose her the way I did. Look what I would have missed. All those years of love, the three most beautiful babies in the world. What if I'd avoided the pain I knew was coming?"

"But wouldn't your crystal ball also have shown you the love and happiness, and the babies?"

"When's the last time you ever heard a fortune teller say, 'I see good times ahead for you'?"

She chuckled at his thick Gypsy accent. "Good point. However, they never predict a woman will meet a man who's short, pale and ugly, either. He's always tall, dark and handsome."

By tacit agreement, the talk did not return to the subject of *we*. They finished their dessert, then drove to a nearby multiplex movie theater. They couldn't decide which movie to see. In the end, they nixed the love story, the romantic comedy, the family Christmas movie, the war epic, and went for the movie with no elements that spoke to their personal situation—a safe, sensible science-fiction action thriller.

It was just their luck that there was a hot, erotic love scene near the end of the movie. The kind of scene that sent hot blood pulsing in intimate places. Riley and Amy both stared studiously at the screen, each making certain not to catch the other's eye. But they would probably have bruises from the tightness of their grip on each other's hand.

They were silent on the way home. Not even the radio broke the humming monotony of tires on blacktop. A casual glance might make someone think that each was off in his or her own little world, paying no attention to the other. And in one respect, that was true. Amy was thinking how much quieter Riley's nice sedan was than her old rattletrap and wishing it wasn't so, for fear that in this quiet car he could hear her swallow, and hear her heart pound. Riley was thinking how lucky he was that the girls were spending the night with Marva and Frank, because he was in absolutely no hurry to go home.

They'd been holding hands since before that steamy scene in the movie. Neither seemed inclined to let go. So they held on. All the way home.

For two single adults on a Saturday-night date, they returned to Amy's apartment at the embarrassingly early hour of eleven o'clock.

For the first time since starting for home, Amy turned her head and looked at Riley. "I don't have anything to offer you to drink, but you're welcome to come up. If you want."

He met her gaze. The dash light and the street light at the end of the parking lot brought an intimacy to the car's interior. "I'd like that." He squeezed her hand gently. "Thanks." His fingers slid away from hers as he opened his door.

All evening he'd been opening doors for her, so she sat still and let him circle the car and help her out. Immediately they clasped hands again, then turned and climbed the stairs together.

Anticipation danced along Amy's nerves. Beside it, fear tried to cut in, but yearning was stronger and pushed it aside. She unlocked her door and they stepped inside her dark apartment.

Riley pushed the door closed behind them.

"It's dark," she said inanely.

He pulled her closer. "You scared?"

Suddenly there didn't seem to be enough air in the room. "No," she told him. "Yes. Maybe. A little."

Holding both of her hands in both of his, he pressed them to his chest. "Me, too."

That was all it took to ease her worries. This

might turn out to be the biggest mistake of her life, but for tonight, it was right.

"Don't worry," she whispered, sidling closer until her breath skimmed his chin. "I'll protect you."

With a low growl, Riley wrapped his arms tightly around her and kissed her. More than kissed, he ravaged, he devoured. She reveled.

"I've been waiting all night to taste you," he murmured as he took his mouth across her cheek, down her neck, back to her lips.

"So have I," she managed on a breath of scarce air. Her entire body felt too big for her skin, as though she might explode any minute. Heat threatened to boil her blood in her veins. She wanted more of him.

As if on cue, they stepped together toward her bedroom door. His jacket and hers fell away while their mouths fused together. When they came up for air they found themselves standing next to her bed.

"I want to see you," he said.

She wanted to see him, too. She turned on the bedside lamp, which cast a circle of light across their legs and half the bed.

With a smile, he threaded his fingers through her hair. "I've never seen it down before."

The feel of his fingers on her scalp and threading through her hair made her groan in pleasure. "I like that."

"I like it, too."

With her eyes closed, she ran her hands up into his hair and smiled. "Like that?"

"Oh, yeah. But I meant I like my hands in your hair, too. But don't stop," he added quickly when she moved as if to take her hands away. "This works for me." He moved his head to press it more firmly into her hands.

Amy opened her eyes and saw him. With his head tilted back, his throat was exposed. She pressed her open mouth against his Adam's apple and tasted his flesh, finding it sharp, salty, tangy. When he moaned, she felt the vibration against her tongue and smiled.

With a twist of his head, he fused his lips to hers again and took her mouth deep and hard. Amy gave him everything she had, and took all he offered, and knew it was too late for her—she was already in love with him.

What came next began as a slow dance of heat and desire that escalated quickly into a rush of fire and nerves, of rasping breath and shaking hands. They kissed and tugged at each other's clothes, letting them land wherever they chose. And they laughed when they had to stop for Riley to tug off his boots. He found it hard to do with Amy trailing open-mouthed kisses across his bare back.

The boots landed with twin *thuds*. Never had Riley been so glad to be rid of them. And never did he remember laughing so much during the removal, or being so thoroughly distracted.

Then he turned to take Amy in his arms and froze. He knew, without asking, what he was seeing. The pale pink scar on her left side, just below her ribs.

With a hand that wanted to tremble, he touched a finger to the scar, felt the extra-thick skin that was part smooth, part puckered. "You left a little something out of the story about that day in Iraq."

Amy flinched slightly at his touch, wondering if he found the scar ugly. She had never cared what it looked like; she had earned it on the field of battle. She straightened her shoulders and stood firm. Let him look. "What should I have said?" she asked him. "Your wife was killed protecting me, but oh, yes, I was shot, too, so let's focus on me, not her?"

"That's not what we would have thought, that you were looking for, what, attention? Sympathy? It would have given us an even clearer picture of how bad it was on that road that day if we'd realized you were injured, too. Was it as bad as it looks? Your wound?"

Amy's tension eased. "It's the only time I was shot, so I don't have anything to compare it to."

He stroked the scar again, and this time she shivered, and not from cold. "It—the bullet didn't hit anything important."

Relief flooded Riley as he pulled her against his chest and wrapped his arms around her. "I'm so glad. So incredibly glad." She felt so good, so right in his arms. So different from the shape and texture he'd been used to, yet so much the same. He knew comparing Amy to Brenda was unfair to both of them, and to him. He let those thoughts fade away and concentrated on the woman in his arms.

She was firm and strong and smelled so sweet. He took her down onto the bed and filled his hands with her, loving the shape of her muscles, and those softer areas. Her breasts fit perfectly in his palms. He trailed his mouth along her jaw and down, lingering to dip his tongue in the hollow of her throat. He liked the way it wobbled when she swallowed.

But he was after plumper game. He kissed his way down the valley between her breasts, then up one slope to the tip. As hard as he already was, the feel of her nipple against his tongue made him harder. He lapped at it, flicked his tongue across it, then settled in and suckled.

Amy arched clear off the bed, the feeling was so exquisite.

Riley growled low in satisfaction. Her responsiveness fed the flames in his gut, pushing him toward the edge. But he wanted to take his time. This feeling of freedom and welcome and sharp arousal was something he wanted to wallow in as long as possible.

He trailed his mouth down the slope of one breast and up to the peak of the other. With his hands he explored the curve of her waist, the flair of her hip, up again to the firmness of her abdomen, feeling it undulate beneath his touch.

The slight scrape of his calloused fingers against her bare flesh took Amy's breath away. She loved those rough, hard hands that were so gentle yet so bold, so arousing. She wanted to feel them everywhere, and she wanted to touch him everywhere.

His skin was so smooth. So hot. She grasped, loving the hard curve of muscle beneath.

His hand on her belly inched lower, lower still.

A small sound escaped her throat. If it sounded like a plea, that's because it was. She wanted this to be as right as it felt. Right for both of them. If a secret fear lived in her heart that they were moving too fast, that this, as wonderful as it was, could lead to disaster, she pushed it away. She wanted his touch. Wanted his hand to move lower, and lower still. And then it did.

His lips traveled over her belly to her side, to the scar earned on a road halfway around the world. His lips and tongue stroked the spot and suddenly she smiled. Who knew a scar from a bullet wound could become an erogenous zone?

His mouth trailed up her torso, along her throat, and settled hungrily over her mouth, while his hand laid gentle siege between her legs. Her hips flexed all on their own, pushing her harder against his hand.

The heat and tension built and built. Her hands slid down his sides and over his taut belly. With one hand she encircled the hard length of him, gratified by the way he sucked in his breath.

"Wait. Wait," he said breathlessly.

"Wha—"

"Protection." He reached toward his jeans on the floor and fished his wallet from the hip pocket.

Amy's mind was in such a fog that it took her a long moment to realize he was getting and donning a condom. She kissed his cheek. "Thank you," she whispered.

He gave her a deep chuckle. "You know what they call a guy who forgets this, don't you?"

She reached down to help him finish rolling the condom into place. "No. What?"

"Daddy."

She looked at him blankly, then, when he smiled, she threw her arms around his waist and burst out laughing. "Is that a fact?"

He nudged her knees apart and settled his hips between her thighs. "I am living proof."

"Then—" He moved, and she gasped. "—I really do thank you."

His grin turned wicked. "You think that's good, just wait."

She laughed again. She had never laughed during sex before. This time with Riley felt so different, so much *more* than she'd ever felt. Inside she knew that she and Riley were not merely having sex. They were making love. And they were laughing.

She felt as if she could fly.

Riley looked down at the glow on her face and the emotion in her eyes and let himself believe that she was his. And then he entered her, and rational thought disappeared.

Amy welcomed the stretching fullness. He seemed to fill her clear up to her heart. Then he eased out, almost all the way, and she felt like weeping until he pushed in again. He withdrew, then filled her, withdrew, filled. Slowly, slowly, slowly, faster, faster, harder, hotter. He took her higher than she'd ever flown. She held on tight and cried out as everything inside her burst free. Colored lights flashed behind her closed eyelids.

A moment later Riley stiffened in her arms. He threw back his head and ground his hips against her. She held him tight and urged him home.

Chapter Nine

Amy regained her wits as she did her breath—
slowly. The warm weight of Riley Sinclair anchored
her where she lay. Was he the anchor she'd been
seeking all her life? The person with whom she
could put down roots?

Her heart, so recently slowed to normal, gave a
leap. She wouldn't make the mistake she'd seen so
many of her friends make, that of thinking one night
of good sex—okay, mind-numbing sex—meant
happily ever after.

She tightened her arms around Riley's shoulders, still not sure of her own emotions, let alone his.

"You're thinking too hard."

She gave a start. "What?"

He pushed himself up onto his forearms and cradled her face in his hands. "I guess I know you better than I thought. Right now you're trying to decide if this means we know what we're doing."

"Home builder, child rearer and now mind reader?" She ran her hands up and down his arms. "Or are you thinking the same thing?"

"I won't be capable of rational thought for a while yet."

She smiled and stared at his chin to avoid looking him in the eyes. "I know what you mean."

"Liar," he said softly as he nuzzled his nose alongside of hers. "Your wheels started turning the minute you caught your breath."

She threaded her fingers together behind his neck. "What makes you think that?"

He kissed her with so much tenderness, she nearly wept. "Because every muscle in your delectable body tensed."

She forced herself to relax. "Is that better?"

"I wasn't complaining," he said. "Just making an

observation." He rolled to his side and took her with him until they were again face to face. "I'm sorry."

"For what?" she asked, her heart aching.

"You didn't deserve to have your thoughts questioned the way I just did."

"Shh." She placed her fingers over his lips. "Let's just forget it, okay?"

"All right." He kissed her once, twice, three times. "We'll start over." He kissed her again, more deeply this time. "Hi. How ya doin'?"

This was better, Amy thought. Don't talk about it. No use in talking about it. Not now, when the glow was still on. And oh, what a glow. "I'm doing fine. More than fine."

He kissed her on the temple, then tucked her head under his chin and hugged her to his chest. "Good. I'm glad."

"Okay, great. I'm glad we cleared that up. We're dynamite in bed together."

"You won't get any argument out of me. But I guess you're wanting to know about out of bed."

"I don't think we've solved anything tonight. I don't think we've answered any questions about what we really feel."

"We answered one."

She heard the smile in his voice. "Are you laughing at me?"

"No. I just don't have an answer for you."

"You don't know if you're just using me to fill Brenda's place, and I don't know if I'm grabbing at some ideal I made up in my mind from the stories Brenda told me."

He pushed her hair away from her face and studied her. "Does it matter? Wait before you answer. I mean, does it really matter right this minute, if we don't understand what the future holds? I don't have any guarantees to offer, Amy. All I know is that tonight, I want you, and you want me. Do we need anything more than that right now?"

Before she could answer, he kissed her. He took her mouth with a fierceness that stunned. She caught fire and matched him, desperate breath for desperate breath. There was no slow buildup this time. They came together in a storm of emotions and physical need so sharp she ached. A yawning emptiness grew inside her. She instinctively knew that no one could ever fill that emptiness for her except Riley.

She welcomed him inside her body and held him close, for those few minutes not caring if there were tomorrows for them, or only tonight. She could live a long time on memories of a night like this. If she didn't completely lose her mind in the flash of heat that engulfed them both.

There was a fierceness to their lovemaking this time, a demand for everything, and they gave it. Heat and madness of passion took over and left no room for thought or worries or what-ifs. There was only the give and take of bodies suddenly slicked with sweat. She met him thrust for thrust, gasp for aching gasp, until the impossibly tight wires inside her snapped and she broke free and soared. And soared again a moment later when he followed her over the edge.

They lay together in each other's arms for some time. It was impossible to tell how long, and Amy had no desire to look at the clock on her bedside table. Eventually they stirred.

He nuzzled the spot just behind her ear. "I have to go," he whispered.

"I know." In a town this small, a local businessman and father of young girls had to mind his reputation. She understood that.

"Do you?" With a finger to the side of her jaw, he turned her head until she faced him. "The girls are with their grandparents, so I'm okay there. But my car's right out there in front of your apartment.

I don't want any talk about you. We're a small, friendly town, but we can be nosy."

She managed a smile. "It's all right, Riley. I know you can't stay."

"Do you know that it's for you, as much as, if not more than for me?"

She stroked the side of his face. "That's sweet."

He snorted and pushed himself up to sit on the side of the bed. "No one's called me sweet in longer than I can remember."

She sat up beside him. "Then shame on them, because it's true."

He grabbed his clothes from the floor and started getting dressed. "Well, don't let it get around. I don't think I'd be much good as a negotiator with my suppliers if they all thought I was sweet."

With a light laugh that cost her more than he would ever know, she crossed to her closet and slipped on a robe. "I see what you mean."

A few minutes later they stood at the door and kissed good night, neither of them trusting the emotions swirling through them.

"We're all right, aren't we?" Riley asked, his voice low and intimate.

She pressed a kiss to his lips. "We're all right."

"Why do I get the feeling that we're not?" He

pulled her close. "Have I rushed things? Was this too soon?"

Amy's stomach clenched. "If it was, you didn't do it alone. I'm the one who invited you up. I knew what would happen. What I hoped would happen."

"Then why do you seem so sad?" he asked with pain in his voice.

"I don't know," she said honestly, tears stinging behind her eyes. "It just all seems too much, you know?"

"Maybe I do," he confessed. "This came on us so fast."

"How can it be real, coming on this fast?" She buried her face against his chest. "I think I'm looking for guarantees, and I know that's crazy. Life doesn't come with guarantees. But…"

"But what? Do you want to take a step back? If you do, you're going to have to say so, because I can't really read your mind, and I don't want to push you into something you're not ready for."

Amy pulled away far enough to be able to look him in the face. "Why do you have to be so agreeable? Here I am, being all wishy-washy, ruining what was just about the most wonderful night of my life—"

"Just about?"

"And you're being all nice and accommodating."

"You want me to complain? Tell you that you're trying to pick apart something that should simply be accepted? Point out that we have feelings for each other, and we should see where they lead us?"

"You aren't worried that they might lead us into a brick wall? That one or the other of us won't end up with our heart ripped to shreds?"

"Well, I wasn't." He released her and ran his hands through his hair in what looked a great deal like a gesture of frustration.

"But you are now?"

"How can I not be? It's a self-fulfilling prophecy."

"What are you talking about?"

"If you worry that something bad will happen, you push and finagle to prevent it and end up causing the very thing you're afraid of. It's like telling yourself not to be nervous. The more you say it, the more nervous you become."

"And you think that's what I'm doing?"

He placed his hands on her shoulders and looked into her eyes solemnly. "I think we just spent an incredible night together. For your information, you are only the second woman I've ever slept with in my life."

She gasped. "Riley—"

"I think we can take these feelings we have for each other and make them into anything we want. We can walk away and never see each other again, or we can stay friends, boss and employee, or we can head into deeper waters and see where they take us. The only thing I ask is that whatever happens or doesn't happen between us not harm my girls."

Amy gaped at him in shock. "That you think you have to say that to me proves how little we know each other. I would *never* harm your girls, not for *anything*."

I think of them as my own, her mind cried out.

And therein lay the crux of her problem. In her heart of hearts, she had thought of the girls and Riley as hers since before she came to town. How could she love a man she'd never met? In truth, Brenda hadn't spoken of him nearly as much as she'd spoken of the girls. It was the girls Amy had loved sight unseen. Had she come to town with the unconscious motive to get close to Riley so she could be close to the girls?

Stunned by this new insight into herself, she could not bring herself to look into Riley's eyes.

"I'm going to be tied up most of the day," Riley said. "So I don't know if I'll be able to call you until late."

She smiled sadly. "You don't need to call me. We'll see each other at the office Monday. I'm not that insecure that I have to hear your voice and know where you are every day." *Ha. Liar.*

"Are you telling me you don't want me to call?"

With a groan and a laugh, Amy shook her head. "I guess I deserved that, but no, that's not what I'm saying. If you want to call me and have time, I'd love to hear from you. If you don't have the time, or merely don't want to call, I promise not to take your lack of calling as a personal rejection. How's that?"

He chuckled. "I think you're right. I think we don't know each other as well as we thought we did. I'm going to leave now, before I make an even bigger ass of myself."

Amy sighed and watched him through her window until he drove out of her parking lot. Then she slid to the floor, exhausted. She had gone from letting Marva's beauty consultant pals poke and prod her that morning, to a thrillingly nervous shopping trip with Riley, to an intimate dinner, an exciting movie, followed by the greatest sex—lovemaking— in her life. Then she'd blown it all by giving voice to insecurities she hadn't realized were so strong.

What was she going to do? Carry on and see what happened? Fall deeper in love with him, then realize all he wanted was someone to take Brenda's place? Any local woman would do for that; he didn't need her.

Yet, he'd chosen her. Why?

Because of her connection with Brenda?

That didn't make sense. There had to be several women in town who had grown up with Riley and Brenda. That kind of shared past would more closely match the life he and Brenda had shared. Just slip another woman in place who had all those same memories, same friends, and, voilà, the perfect match.

The memories Amy held of Brenda did not include Riley. They were of months of life in a war zone, no matter what the politicians called it. A little fun, a ton of work, a considerable amount of danger. They were of bullets and terror and blood. And death.

Why would Riley want to keep those memories around his daughters or himself? Sure he wanted to know of them, but that didn't mean he needed her around as a constant reminder.

Around and around the thoughts raced through her mind, like a hamster on an exercise wheel. They plagued her the rest of the night, keeping her from any semblance of sleep. She didn't know how to slow them down or get them off the damn wheel.

* * *

Amy wasn't the only one who couldn't sleep the rest of that night. Riley, too, lay awake and wondered what had gone wrong. Amy hadn't seemed like the insecure type. She had been confident and assertive from the day he'd met her. At work she stood toe to toe with his suppliers and crews and easily held her own. She had even managed to deal effectively with Marva.

So what had gone wrong tonight? She'd been his. He'd felt it in every kiss, every touch. It had felt so damn real. And then, he'd felt her go from limp with pleasure to tense in an instant. The instant her mind had clicked into gear again.

She thought he wanted someone—anyone—to take Brenda's place.

There was no wrong or right response to that. Brenda had been his wife, and, yes, eventually he would probably want to remarry. But no, he didn't want a carbon copy of Brenda. She'd been one of a kind. He had loved her with all his heart. No one could take that away or replace her. But there was room in his heart to love another woman. It didn't have to take anything away from what he'd felt for Brenda. He wouldn't let it.

He'd thought, hoped, that Amy might be the

one. She'd surprised him, because he hadn't been ready to think about a new woman in his life yet. When thoughts of a new woman had sifted through his mind, it had always been for the future. Years away from now.

And yet, there she'd stood, on his front porch that morning. Then she was in his home. At the café. At his dinner table. In the lens of his camera. In his office. Shopping for Christmas presents for his daughters. And finally, tonight, beneath him, surrounding him, sheathing him, burning him alive in her bed.

Then, *kablooey*. The what-ifs and do-you-thinks came sneaking into bed with them.

He supposed he had to bear his share of the blame. He'd felt her tense beneath him and had guessed what she was thinking, but he could have kept his mouth shut. But no, not him. Get it out in the open and talk about it. Hash it out so there were no misunderstandings.

Yeah. Right.

He should have kept his mouth shut.

On the other hand, he thought with resignation, if Amy was so worried about their inner motives that she could end up sabotaging their relationship—if they could call what they had a relationship—he was better off knowing it now rather than later.

He was no closer to a resolution in his mind the next morning when he drove to Marva and Frank's after church to have Sunday dinner and bring the girls home.

"Daddy, Daddy," the girls cried.

"There's my girls." He dropped to one knee and held out his arms to pull them close. It wasn't the first night they'd spent away from him, but it hadn't happened often enough for him or them to be used to it.

"Riley." Marva came to the living room from the kitchen, wiping her hands on a dish towel. "You're just in time. Dinner is almost ready. Girls, go wash your hands. Frank, help the girls wash up while Riley tells me about his evening."

"Nothing to tell. We had a good time. I appreciate you keeping the girls."

"You're welcome, but you're going to have to do better than 'a good time.' This was a monumental event."

Riley pursed his lips and went to the sink to wash his hands. "You don't know the half of it," he muttered.

"Meaning?"

He wasn't about to talk about his sex life with his former mother-in-law. "Meaning, this is the first time I've been out with any woman other than Brenda."

"Of course it is, dear. It's barely been a year since we lost her. Any sooner would have—"

"Ever," he stated.

"Pardon?"

"Sugarpie." Frank stepped into the kitchen. "Don't pester the boy."

"I'm not pestering him."

"Good," Frank said heartily. "Here's our girls."

Pammy, Jasmine and Cindy trouped into the room.

"We're hungry enough we could eat a whole herd of horses, aren't we, girls?"

"Oh, Gramps," Jasmine and Pammy laughed.

Cindy giggled, then hiccuped.

They made it through Marva's delicious pot roast with no more questions about Riley's date, for which he was grateful. After dinner he offered to help Marva clean up, but, as usual, she wouldn't hear of it. She was just old-fashioned enough to consider that women's work. For which Frank was grateful.

As soon as he could manage it without being rude, Riley got the girls to gather up their belongings and took them home, where there was no such thing as women's work. He had several loads of laundry to do.

That evening, while the girls watched a Disney video, Riley slipped off to his bedroom for privacy and phoned Amy.

When the phone rang, Amy jerked as if shot. She reached out for the receiver, then yanked her hand back and held it against her chest to keep from reaching again. It could only be Riley. No one else even knew her, really.

For that matter, she didn't seem to know herself, she thought with a harsh laugh.

Was this love? Or a continuation of the envy she'd felt for months and months, since she'd first heard Brenda talk about her wonderful husband and children?

She wasn't ready to talk to him. She didn't know what to say. So she sat on her sofa and tried not to let the guilt eat her alive.

And dammit, why did she feel guilty for not answering her own phone, anyway? She didn't have to answer her phone if she didn't want to, did she?

So why, she wondered with an aching heart, did it feel like lying?

By the time she went to work the next morning her nerves were on meltdown and her eyes were red and puffy.

"Come on, Galloway," she muttered as she threw her bag beneath her desk and powered up her computer. "Soldier up and quit acting like an indecisive ninny."

Easy for you to say. In Iraq I'm brave and smart. In Tribute, Texas, I'm a stupid twit.

"Good morning."

She barely bit back the shriek that threatened at the scare his voice gave her when she hadn't realized he'd come in. "Good morning," she managed. She stared at her computer screen and typed in her password to log on.

His footsteps crossed from the door to her desk. He stopped there. "I called you last night," he said quietly.

Amy's stomach clenched. "Did you?"

"Several times."

She could see his hand resting on the edge of her desk. "I must have been out." Heaven help her, she'd turned into a liar, she thought with dismay.

"Amy, will you look at me?"

She had to. She knew she had to. She even wanted to. Maybe. Sort of. She swallowed, wishing she knew what to do, what she wanted, what was best for them. If there was a *them*.

Slowly she raised her gaze. "Riley, I..."

"Don't, Amy. If it's this hard for you even to look at me, I guess we have a bigger problem than moving too fast."

"I'm sorry. I don't know what to say. I don't know what to do. I'm driving myself crazy here."

He held her gaze for a long moment. "Are you going to push me away?"

"You mean I haven't already?"

"No, you haven't. I'm harder to push than that. You've asked for some room, some time. Is that what you want?"

"Is time and room supposed to make things clear to me?"

"Are you saying you don't want— You just want to call it quits between us right now?"

Amy felt the blood drain from her face. Was that what she wanted? To call it quits between them? She gave him a sad smile. "Is this your idea of giving me time?"

"I just—" He waved one arm toward her, then ran his fingers through his hair in frustration. "I said I'd call, so I called."

"Is that what this is about? I didn't answer my phone?"

"I think I should go out and come in again so we can start this day over."

"Maybe you should go out and not come in again," she muttered.

"What was that?"

She sighed. "Can we drop it?"

"All of it? Drop us?"

Amy wanted to scream. She could put enough pressure on herself, thank you very much. She didn't need this from him. "I can't do this."

"I'm not sure I can, either." He stared at her, then headed for the door. "I'm going out to check on the jobs."

By Wednesday things were no better between Riley and Amy. He was still avoiding the office as much as possible and she was still barely speaking to him. His crews at the three job sites he had working that week in town were getting paranoid over his constant presence.

To add to his misery, on Tuesday the weather had decided to play with them. The temperature rose to fifty and brought a downpour, leaving the bare ground at his job sites a mess of mud. This particular site, the Cantrells' new ranch house seven miles from town, still had problems with runoff. As soon as the ground was dry enough, they would have to fire up the grader and take care of that.

Maybe this thick gumbo sticking to his boots and everything else that touched it would keep his mind off the woman in his office back in town. She was a crackerjack employee, but not much in the relationship department.

Terrific. It was raining again. Just what he needed. At least this time it was a light rain. He climbed into his pickup and headed back down the gravel road toward the pavement that would take him to town.

Of course, the one romantic relationship he'd been involved in had been the success of his life. Maybe just because Amy didn't love him the way Brenda had didn't mean there was nothing there for the two of them to build on.

Hell. What made him think he was due a second love anyway? Who needed it?

He'd been focused so hard on chasing Amy out of his head that he hadn't noticed the drop in temperature. Halfway down the gravel road the light rain turned to sleet. By the time he reached the two-lane blacktop highway that led to town the road was covered in a thin sheet of black ice. A healthy instinct for preservation pulled his attention from his troubled love life to the dangerous road conditions.

It seemed that everyone but him had sense enough to stay off the roads this afternoon, as he didn't see a single car. But two miles from town, just before the Soldier Creek Bridge, he did see a deer. A big, beautiful twelve-point buck leapt from the brush on his right and sprang onto the road directly in front of Riley.

As mindful of the ice as he could be, yet aware that hitting the animal head-on would kill the deer and could kill himself, too, Riley swerved.

The pickup went into a skid. When the tires left the pavement and dug into the soft shoulder, the truck rolled over. The ditch rushed up to meet the windshield. Riley had a quick vision of his life. It wasn't the past that left him wanting, but the lonely future stretching out ahead. If he lived.

He had one final thought before his head crashed against the side window—*Amy*.

By four forty-five that afternoon Amy had reached a shattering decision. She could not continue to face Riley every day as long as there was this awful tension between them. Since no resolution to the tension seemed near, she was going to have to find herself another job.

She wouldn't leave him flat. Business was slow during winter weather like this, she reminded herself as she looked out the window at the ice building up on every surface out there. It wasn't as if her presence was critical to his success. But she would stay at least until Fanny came back after the first of the year.

The decision eased the tension in her shoulders, but left her incredibly sad. But it was for the best that she leave. He would be relieved, she was sure.

When the phone rang, she welcomed the distraction. "Sinclair Construction."

"This is County Deputy Will Sanchez. Is this Amy Galloway?"

"It is. What can I do for you, Deputy?"

"Ma'am, there's been an accident."

Chapter Ten

All the way to the hospital on the hill at the south edge of town Amy kept her mind blank. She couldn't allow herself to think. She scarcely allowed herself to breathe. An accident. Riley. Deer. Truck. Ditch. The words hurled themselves at her one after the other, like heat-seeking missiles.

At the last stop sign before the hill, she hit her brakes too hard and her tires slid across the intersection. She was lucky no other cars were coming. She held her breath until the car straightened out, then eased up the hill and skated into the parking lot of the hospital.

With a prayer on her lips, she rushed into the hospital and demanded to see Riley.

They told her she should sit down. They told her it shouldn't be long. They told her she had to wait.

She told them, "Point me toward Riley Sinclair right this minute and you might live to see the end of your shift."

"Security!"

"Oh, for heaven's sake," Amy said as she started down the hall. "If you've got a security guard here in the middle of the day I'll kiss somebody's backside." She followed the sound of voices into an exam room.

In the doorway, she froze. "Riley." Her heart jumped into her throat. He sat on the end of the exam table, one shoe missing and that pant leg ripped open to the knee. Bloody scratches crisscrossed the flesh visible through the tear, and more scratches marred the backs of his hands.

"Hold that right here and press." An elderly man in a white lab coat directed Riley's hand to the gauze pad at the side of his head. The doctor then turned toward the counter behind him.

Amy swallowed around the lump of terror threatening to choke her. "Riley, what happened? Are you all right? How bad is it?" She rushed to his side.

"Amy." Riley held one arm out for her while using his other hand to hold the gauze pad in place. His face was streaked with blood and scratches.

"I'm all right, just a little cut on the head."

They stared at each other for a moment, then he pulled her hard against his chest. With a small sob, she went willingly.

"I was so scared. All they said was you'd had an accident and the ambulance took you to the hospital. I didn't know what to think."

"I'm sorry." He clasped her tight and kissed her temple, her cheek. "I'm sorry you were scared. Don't be scared."

Still frantic, she touched his face, every place she could find that didn't look as if it hurt. His eyebrows. One cheek. His nose. "I'm so sorry I pushed you away."

"No, no, I'm sorry." His hungry eyes searched every inch of her face. "I shouldn't have rushed you."

"No, you should have. I was being silly, and that's not like me."

"When the truck rolled into the ditch, all I could think was that I let you go too easily. I shouldn't have let you push me away. I shouldn't have pushed you away. I should have fought for you, for us. I don't want to scare you off."

She choked back a sob of relief. "You couldn't scare me off after this with a Howitzer."

He squeezed her so hard with one arm that she feared her ribs would crack, but she didn't care. She didn't want him ever to let go of her. But she was afraid to squeeze him too hard until she knew the extent of his injuries.

She pushed back slightly. "How bad's your head? What about your leg?"

"I'm fine," he told her. "Just a few scratches."

A disgusted "Hmph" came from the doctor at the counter behind them.

Amy narrowed her eyes at Riley. "What aren't you telling me?"

He grimaced. "It's no big deal. I just need a couple of stitches, that's all. Then I'm outta here."

"Six," came the doctor's voice. "And you should spend the night for observation."

Amy's fear eased into concern. He wasn't going to die from his injuries, but he was banged up enough to cause some damage. "What else, Doctor?" she asked.

The doctor turned and started cleaning the gash on Riley's head.

"You're not going to shave a bald spot, are you?" Riley asked warily.

"Hush up," Amy told him. "If he needs to shave a bald spot, you'll let him."

"Yes, ma'am."

"Oh," the doctor said with an arched brow. "So that's the way the wind blows, huh? Can you get him to stay the night?"

Amy swallowed. "What would be the purpose?"

"I'd like to keep an eye on him, make sure he doesn't develop any problems from this mild concussion he's given himself."

"Hey, don't blame me," Riley protested. "Go talk to that twelve-point buck I swerved to miss."

Ignoring Riley, Amy looked to the doctor. "I can check on him during the night."

"Every few hours? Make sure he knows who and where he is? And when?"

"I can do that," she promised. "Better that than scare his daughters to death. They just lost their mother last year. If their father ends up in the hospital, well, I don't think we should put them through that if we don't have to."

Riley threaded his fingers through hers and looked at her with deep gratitude. "Thank you. I'm kinda surprised Marva hasn't swooped down on me yet."

"My fault. I knew she had the girls with her so I told the deputy not to call over there, that I'd take care of it."

Riley smiled. "My brave soldier."

"Not at all," she admitted. "Just selfish. I wanted to get my hands on you first. I'll get you situated at home, then I'll go over there and tell them what's happened and bring the girls home. It'll make them feel better if they get to help take care of you."

"That sounds workable," the doctor said. "I'll look that leg over, then write you a script for antibiotics and a pain killer, because this head is going to pound like a bass drum."

"It already is," Riley confessed.

Amy pestered Riley to tell her what happened while the doctor finished suturing his head. He told her about the deer, about swerving, about ending up upside-down in the ditch.

Amy shuddered at how easily he could have been killed. Or died of hypothermia or exposure if someone hadn't found him before night. "What happened to Bambi?" she asked.

"Bambi's dad. I missed him. He ran off. Man, he was a beauty."

"He needs to stay off the road," she said with a low growl. "He nearly killed you."

"We're even. I nearly killed him, too."

* * *

Amy would have taken Riley straight home from the hospital as planned, but he argued, successfully, that it would be a waste of time. They instead drove to the drug store and filled his prescriptions. Next they went to the Greens' to get the girls. To get the worst of the day's events behind him, he went to the door and presented himself, bloodstained, torn and stitched as he was, so Marva and Frank could see for themselves that he was fine. More or less.

Amy went in with him, mainly to guard her place at his side and prevent Marva from taking over his care.

Possessive? Yes. Petty? Who cared?

When all the fuss died down, Amy stepped in and steered Riley and his girls out the door. She drove them all straight home and got them into the house quickly. She sent Riley to his bathroom to clean up, then turned to his daughters.

"Okay, girls, you're going to have to help me take care of your daddy," she told them.

They lined up side by side and stared up at her solemnly.

"Hey, don't look so serious. Your daddy's not hurt very badly."

"Our momma got hurt," Jasmine said.

"And she died," Cindy added.

"I know she did, sweetie, but your daddy's not hurt that way. He just bumped his head when he wrecked his pickup. He's not going to die from it. But he's going to be sore, and his cuts and scrapes are going to hurt."

"Can we put bandages on them?" Jasmine asked.

"We sure can," Amy said.

Cindy sniffled. "I don't want Daddy to be hurt."

"Neither do I," Amy said. "So we'll have to take really good care of him, won't we?"

"I'll get first aid supplies," Pammy said. "I know what to get."

"Okay, bring them to the den. We'll let him sit in his recliner while we doctor him," Amy suggested. She craned her neck to peer down the hall. Seeing no sign of Riley, she led the girls a few feet away into the kitchen and gave them a conspiratorial wink.

"Here's the deal, girls. Your daddy's barely hurt at all. No more than one of you falling off your bicycle and getting a few scrapes."

Pammy poked out her lower lip. "Are you sure?"

"I'm sure. I was there in the hospital when the doctor checked him over. He does have stitches on the side of his head, but not much else. But the thing is, guys are different than girls. Guys are bigger and stronger than we are. At the same time, when they get the least little scrape, or catch a cold, they turn into helpless babies. They need help with every little thing."

That got a round of smiles out of the girls.

"I'm telling you this so you won't worry about your daddy just because he moans and groans now and then over his aches and pains. It's just that helpless baby inside the big man. He can't help it. Now, here's the rule. If you like the guy, or love him, you let him get away with it."

"What do you mean?" Pammy asked, a look of outrage on her nine-year-old face.

"I mean we get them a drink of water, or a tissue, or a sandwich or whatever will make them feel better. They're always there for us, so once in a while, like when they get a boo-boo or stitches on their head—"

"Or a cold," Cindy added.

"Yes, or a cold. When that happens, we take care of them. Got it?"

"I guess," Pammy said.

The other two girls nodded.

"Okay, let's go take care of your daddy."

* * *

Riley's accident wasn't nearly as overwhelming as the relief he felt that Amy had come for him. It wasn't over between them. If he had his way, it might never be. And bless her for taking care of him and the girls tonight.

He showered away the blood and mud and muck and tugged on a pair of clean jeans and a flannel shirt. Barefoot, he made his way back to the den and his girls. All four of them, he thought with awareness. He just needed a way to make certain the fourth one didn't try to bolt on him again.

They were waiting for him. He was in for it. They held cotton balls, hydrogen peroxide, bandages. His youngest wore her toy stethoscope around her neck. He bit back a bark of laughter; he wouldn't hurt her feelings for the world, and she looked dead earnest.

"Welcome to our clinic," Amy told him. "Your personal staff of nurses is here to help you. But, sir, how are we supposed to doctor that leg if you're wearing jeans?"

Riley arched his brow. "You want me to take off my pants?"

Amy's eyes widened. She mashed her lips together.

Three little girls giggled. One of them followed with a hiccup.

"Could you put on a pair of shorts, or a robe, until we're finished?"

Riley chuckled and started toward the kitchen. "My leg's fine. But my stomach is empty."

"No, Daddy, we have to doctor you." Cindy planted herself before him, her tiny fists propped on her hips. "You're s'posed to be helpless."

When all was said and done, Riley was once more in his jeans and flannel shirt, but his leg, arm and face bore bandages with purple dinosaurs on them. Amy had thrown together a supper of soup, salad and toast. Riley had drawn the line at letting Nurse Esmeralda feed him the soup one drizzling spoonful at a time, but to make up for it, he let her sit on his lap during the girls' half hour of television. She had kept her stethoscope pressed to his chest and listened to his heartbeat during the entire program.

By the time Amy had helped him tuck the girls in bed and he'd read to them for a few minutes, he was starting to feel the effects of the wreck. Every muscle in his body ached. His skin ached. His head, well, he couldn't think of a word stronger than *pounded*, but *pounded* didn't begin to describe it.

"Here." Amy held out a glass of water and two pills from his prescription bottles.

"Reading my mind?" He downed the pills and the water.

"Just the color of your skin. You're looking a little pale."

He gave her a brief smile. "It's the purple dinosaurs. They do it to me every time. Come here." He pulled her close and rested his cheek on the top of her head. "Thank you for taking care of us tonight. I don't know what I'd have done without you."

Alarmed at how heavily he leaned on her, Amy braced herself beneath his arm. "You would have managed. Come on. I bet you're ready for bed."

He let her steer him down the hall toward his bedroom. "Are you coming with me?"

"I'm right here, aren't I?"

"No, no, no, I mean are you coming to bed with me?"

Amy smiled. Those pills were starting to work already. He was sounding like a petulant three-year-old. "Don't worry about me. I'm going to take care of you."

"Yeah," he said, staggering against the doorway to his room. "But are you going to *take care* of me?"

She looked up at his face to see him jerking his

eyebrows up and down, making two of the Barneys look as though they were dancing. She tried to swallow the bubble of laughter that rose in her so as not to disturb the girls just down the hall, but it came out as a snicker. "I think those pills are making you loopy. Come on, to bed with you."

She managed to pull the covers and his jeans down and get him seated on the side of the bed without tumbling them both to the floor. But he turned the tables on her and put his arm around her waist and tumbled them both onto his bed. His head landing against the mattress defeated his amorous intentions.

"Ow," he cried.

"You have to be careful," she cautioned.

"You coulda warned me."

Again with the three-year-old pout. Amy smiled. "I'm sorry." She scrambled free of his arms and legs and climbed from the bed. Finally she got him turned around so that his head lay cushioned on the pillow and the covers were pulled up to his chin. "You can sleep now," she told him. "But I'll be back in a little while to check on you."

"Don't leave me." His voice was fading. His eyes slid shut. "Stay with me."

She waited, one breath, two, three. He was sound asleep. She leaned over and kissed him between dinosaurs. "I'm not going anywhere," she whispered.

Nowhere farther than the other end of the hall. For this night, at least. She wasn't going to look for trouble down the road. One day, and night, at a time. She could do that.

In the den she found a recent paperback bestselling mystery novel. Marveling that Riley could ever find time to sit and read, she settled into his chair and opened it.

Every couple of hours she returned to Riley's bedside and woke him. "Who am I?" she asked.

"Go away," he muttered the first time.

"What's my name?" she insisted.

"Sergeant Amy. I have purple dinosaurs on my face and stitches in my head. I know who and where I am, and I'm going back to sleep now."

"Okay, sleep." She kissed his cheek and straightened the covers over his chest, but he never knew. He'd already gone back to sleep.

The next time, she made him tell her the date and the names of his daughters.

The third time she woke him he threatened to strangle her. "If you're going to wake me up all night long, at least give me the pleasure of holding you." He tugged on her arm and pulled her off balance, making her fall on top of him. They both let out a muffled *oomph*.

"There." He let out a deep sigh. "That's better."

As much as Amy wanted to accommodate him and fall asleep draped across his chest or curled up in his arms, she knew she couldn't allow herself the luxury. Not with three little girls just down the hall. She wasn't prepared for the consequences— and she was sure that neither was Riley—of having his daughters wake up and find her in bed with their father.

Oh, no, that wouldn't do at all.

She pushed herself off the bed, gave him another kiss, this one on the mouth, and lingering, then escaped to the den again. At least she could let him sleep for several hours this time, according to the doctor's instructions. Which meant that she could get some sleep herself. She stretched out on the couch and closed her eyes.

"Should we wake her up?"

"No."

"I think we should wake her up."

Back and forth the loud whispers went, penetrating Amy's brain, forcing their way into her sleep.

She'd had the oddest dream. She dreamed she'd fallen asleep on Riley's couch.

Riley's couch!

She sprang upright, blinking her eyes open.

Three little girls shrieked and jumped back.

Wiping his hands on a dish towel, Riley ambled into the sunlit room from the kitchen. "You're awake." He smiled.

"I am?" Amy scanned the room to orient herself and give her brain time to catch up with her body.

"Daddy says he's not helpless anymore," Cindy pronounced. "He says he's all better now."

"He does, does he?" Amy looked Riley up and down. He looked delicious in those jeans and that plaid flannel shirt. It was the bare feet that made her pulse leap. Especially the one with the purple dinosaur bandage.

He had removed most of the bandages on his face so he could shave, but he'd left the two on his forehead. He was being a good sport, not wanting to make the girls think their care and attention hadn't been needed.

What a man, she thought dreamily.

"Oatmeal is on the table," he announced.

During breakfast Riley told Amy he was staying home with the girls that day, since they were out of school for the rest of the week for Christmas vacation.

"I assume you want the office open," she said.

"I don't see why," he said. "Just put a message on the answering machine saying we're closed until January second, but if there's an emergency they can reach me at home, and put my number on there."

She smiled. "The joys of owning your own business in a small town."

After breakfast Amy gathered her coat and bag to go home. Riley walked her toward the door and made no effort to hide from the girls when he pulled her beneath the mistletoe and kissed her socks off.

"Well," she managed when he let her up for air. "I guess you are feeling better."

"Much, thanks to you." He kissed her again, this time with enough tenderness to make her heart hope.

Chapter Eleven

The rest of the week until Christmas passed in a blur. Amy spent much of it with Riley and his girls.

There were errands to run. There was more shopping to do, both in town and beyond. There were videos to rent and watch and a movie to see in Waco. There were friends and neighbors to meet.

Amy wondered what those friends and neighbors thought of Riley showing up with her, but they were all friendly. They were especially nice when Riley told them that she had served with Brenda. That served as a good, acceptable reason for them to be together without too much overt speculation.

They were seldom alone, she and Riley. There was little time for it with the girls always around. But Amy didn't mind. There was always time for a few heated kisses when they weren't looking, or after their bedtime if Amy drove herself home.

She had her own last-minute Christmas things to take care of, too. Things she could not do around Riley or his girls. But with a few phone calls, a quick trip here and there, they were quickly done and now waited only for the arrival of the big day.

Finally it was Christmas Eve. When it came time to put out the cookies and milk for Santa—and a handful of alfalfa pellets for the reindeer—Riley made certain that Amy shared in the ritual. Every minute, she fell deeper and harder for this man.

She had agreed to help Riley put together the toys and things that would come from Santa. He had warned her it could take all night, and it did. Bicycles, a doll house, a new computer and everything else three young girls could want.

Amy brought in the three wrapped boxes she had put together for Brenda and placed them against the wall, in the back of all the other presents. She didn't want the girls tearing into them, then moving on to the next toy or game. She wanted them to focus on what their mother had chosen for them. She knew it was a lot to ask of three young children on Christmas morning, but Riley thought that they would be tired enough after opening everything else that they wouldn't have any trouble sitting still for a few minutes.

And so it went. She and Riley barely got everything situated before the bedroom door flew open and three shrieking little girls came racing down the hall toward the tree.

At the last second, she watched Riley turn his back and block the view of the snack they'd left out for their North Pole visitors. When he turned back around, the milk was gone, and only a few crumbs remained of the cookies. She didn't want to know what had become of the alfalfa pellets.

The girls never noticed a thing. They were too busy finding and tearing into all their presents. Watching them was both magical and exhausting.

It didn't take long before almost all the packages were opened. Riley had his share, too, from the girls. Marva had obviously helped them pick out the socks, shirt and tie. Then there were the homemade gifts of glittered hand prints, macaroni-covered pop bottles, finger paintings and the like. Amy could tell by the love in his eyes that he treasured each gift and its giver.

There were gifts for Amy, too, much to her surprise. She got her very own finger painting and macaroni bottle, plus a set of hand prints highlighted in silver glitter, and from Riley, a beautiful silk scarf in swirls of bold colors.

"Thank you," Amy said with feeling. "All of you. I wasn't expecting any of this."

"Merry Christmas," Pammy said.

"Yes," Riley added. "Merry Christmas." And right there in front of the girls, with the mistletoe clear across the room, he leaned over and kissed her. On the mouth.

The girls giggled.

Then it was time. Riley brought the three large boxes from against the wall.

"What's this?" he asked, finding a large wrapped rectangle behind the boxes.

"That's yours," Amy said.

"From you? Wow."

"Partly from me, partly from Brenda."

"Oh?"

"Yes. You can save it for after the girls open theirs."

That was all the permission the girls needed.

They tore into their boxes. Each one pulled out the backpack featuring their favorite cartoon character.

"First," Amy said, "you'll each find a letter from your mother. It's the same letter in each of your packs, so, Riley, why don't you read it to them?"

"No." He shook his head and cleared his throat. "This is your gig. You read it."

"All right. It says, 'My Darling Daughters: I'm so sorry I couldn't be there with you for Christmas, but it is beyond my control. Know that I love you and am thinking of you, and wishing I was there. I've put together a few items for you as my Christmas present. First is one videotape for you to share. I put it in Pammy's package. It shows you where I live here, my barracks, that sort of thing. Then there's a different videotape in each of your packs. On each one, I am reading one of your favorite stories. So now I can read to you any time you want.'"

The girls cried out and dug into their packs, pulling out their videotapes.

"'I've also written separate letters that are private, one for each of you. Cindy, Jasmine, your daddy can help you read yours. Then you'll each find a small plastic bag with some items inside. These, too, are from me to you: there's a pencil to remind you to do your homework, a lipstick kiss from me to you on a piece of pink paper, a dollar bill, in case your allowance runs out, an eraser, because mistakes are okay, as long as you correct them and a bandage that I've already kissed, in case you get a boo-boo. And there you have it, a few things to remember me by. I love you so much. Merry Christmas, sweethearts.'"

The girls were holding their plastic bags and reciting what each item was for.

"Wow," Riley said. "She put some thought into these things, didn't she?"

"A lot of thought. You can open yours now," Amy suggested.

"I'm almost afraid to."

Amy put her hand over his and squeezed. "I understand. But open it anyway."

"Open yours, Daddy," Pammy said.

"Yeah," the other girls chimed in.

Knowing he was probably going to lose it any minute and scare his girls to death by breaking down and crying, Riley took a deep breath, hoping it might steady his emotions. It didn't seem to help, so he pulled the paper off his present. He held it up, and sucked in a sharp breath.

He was going to need that breath, because he wasn't sure he would ever be able to breathe again.

"How…? When…?"

"Brenda had the photo with her. She knew she wanted to do something, but all she could think of was to blow it up. I ran across a guy on the Internet who does oil paintings from photos. I thought she would like that."

"What is it, Daddy?" Jasmine asked.

He couldn't move.

"It's us," Pammy cried. "Mama and us girls in the backyard."

It had always been one of Riley's favorite pictures of Brenda and the girls. In fact he had a copy of it right now in his wallet. Brenda, sitting in the grass, with Pammy and Jasmine on either side and Cindy in her lap. He had taken the picture himself just before Brenda shipped out, nearly two years ago.

The artist had enlarged it and copied it in oil. It was perhaps the most beautiful portrait he'd ever seen. His vision blurred.

"Lemme see, Daddy, lemme see," Cindy cried.

When he finally looked up at Amy, he didn't know what to say.

She leaned toward him and kissed each of his eyelids, then his mouth. "Merry Christmas, Riley."

Amy was gratified by the pleasure the girls and Riley got from the gifts she'd brought them from Brenda. Riley hung the painting in the den—Brenda's great room—where they could see it every day.

"Will you mind seeing her up there every time you come over?" he asked her.

The girls had approved the hanging and were now getting dressed to go to Nana's for Christmas dinner.

Amy smiled at him. "Riley, I see her every time I look at you or any one of your daughters. She's been the biggest, and dare I say, best part of your life for all of your life, and she was my best friend. I can never mind or resent or dislike anything about her. Which reminds me—I have one more thing. Wait just a minute."

While she dug in her bag for the small box hidden there, she called the girls back to the den. Alerted by the excitement in her voice, they raced from their room to see what was happening. They were already dressed for Nana's, except for their shoes.

"I don't know how I could have forgotten," Amy said when they were all gathered in the den. "The finishing touch." She opened the box and presented them with Brenda's green ceramic mama frog that belonged with the collection on the bookshelf. "Your mother's frog is home."

"Oh, wow," Pammy said.

"That's cool," Jasmine said.

"Yeah, cool," Cindy added.

None of the girls seemed overly impressed. They all smiled and carefully stroked the green frog, then they dashed back to their room for their shoes.

That fast, Amy and Riley were alone again.

He took her shoulders in his hands. "Have I ever told you that I love you?"

Amy froze. If it was possible to freeze while heat suffused her skin. "No." She swallowed. Her hands shook. Her knees turned watery. "I don't believe you have."

"Well don't let it scare you away," he said softly. "Just know it's there when you want it."

"We're ready, Daddy. Is Amy going with us?"

"Oh, I—"

Riley cut her off. "Of course she is."

Ah ha, she thought, eager for something, anything else to focus on other than the bombshell he'd just dropped on her. Christmas at the in-laws. And they weren't even her in-laws.

But they welcomed her cordially, and no wonder. She was just one more among the horde that descended on the Green household that day. Both of their sons, plus wives and children, had come for the day from where they were stationed in San Antonio.

Halfway through dinner, when she thought she could reasonably gain the attention of all of the adults, Amy cleared her throat and tapped her knife against her glass.

"May I have your attention, please?" As soon as everyone stopped talking, she spoke. "I have a gift to present to all of you, but it has to be done tomorrow afternoon."

"What are you talking about?" Riley asked.

"I'd like all of you to meet me in Tribute Park at two o'clock tomorrow. And that's all I'm going to say."

"What have you done?" Riley asked her.

She smiled. "You'll see."

Of course, given the location and her secrecy, there wasn't much doubt as to what her surprise was.

"You've done something on the Tribute Wall," Frank said. "But that doesn't make sense. Brenda's already on the War Memorial."

"That doesn't mean she couldn't be on the Tribute Wall," Marva said. "Does it?"

It didn't, as they all found out the next day.

A small crowd gathered. The entire Green family, Riley and his girls, several dozen townspeople and some uniformed soldiers that no one but Amy seemed to know.

The mayor did the honors, calling everyone to attention near the tarp that covered the new section of granite, then quickly turned the mike over to Amy.

"Thank you all for coming here today. A new name has been added to the Tribute Wall to honor a local person who has gone above and beyond the call of duty and made the ultimate sacrifice so that others might live. I'm speaking of Brenda Green Sinclair, Sergeant, U.S. Army National Guard."

Amy told the story of Brenda's deeds that day in Iraq, of the lives she saved, of the way she died.

"Her selfless act of courage saved the lives of four of her fellow soldiers, myself included. Ladies and gentlemen, I give you a tribute to Brenda Sinclair."

At her nod, the tarp was pulled away to reveal the newly etched granite panel. It listed Brenda's name, rank, the dates of her birth and death, location of her death, and the names of the people she saved.

"Joining me today to pay tribute to Sergeant Sinclair are Corporals Johnson and Cohen and Private First Class Don Meeker, none of whom would be alive today if not for Brenda. And also here today is Captain Enrique Lopez, who has a special presentation to make to Brenda's husband."

Riley stood, stunned, as he was presented with a Bronze Star in Brenda's name, in recognition of her act of bravery.

Then everyone was congratulating him and the Greens and slapping each other on the back. He shook hands with the soldiers, the townspeople, probably a stranger or two. He wasn't sure exactly what happened during those next several minutes, he was so stunned.

"You did all this," he finally managed to say to Amy.

Amy swallowed. It was now or never. While Marva and Frank and their sons, along with Brenda's daughters, all looked on.

"I did, yes," she said clearly. "I did it to honor Brenda. I never want to take her place. I couldn't if I tried. Instead, I want my own place in your life and in the lives of your daughters, because I love you, all of you, very much. I would be honored to be the one to see that your daughters never forget their mother. If you'll have me, Riley, I would very much like to be the new wife and mother of the Sinclair family. Will you marry me?"

Riley's grin came slowly and spread wide. "What do you say, girls? Should we marry her?"

"Yes!"

"Yeah!"

"Yea!"

"All right, then," he said, his eyes never leaving Amy's. "It's unanimous. We accept."

A loud cheer went up throughout the crowd.

* * * * *

*Experience entertaining women's fiction
for every woman who has wondered
"what's next?" in their lives.
Turn the page for a sneak preview
of a new book from Harlequin NEXT,
WHY IS MURDER ON THE MENU, ANYWAY?
by Stevi Mittman*

On sale December 26, wherever books are sold.

Design Tip of the Day

Ambience is everything. Imagine eating a foie gras at a luncheonette counter or a side of coleslaw at Le Cirque. It's not a matter of food but one of atmosphere. Remember that when planning your dining room design.

—Tips from *Teddi.com*

"Now that's the kind of man you should be looking for," my mother, the self-appointed keeper of my shelf-life stamp, says. She points with her fork at a man in the corner of the Steak-Out Restaurant, a dive I've just been hired to redecorate. Making this restaurant look four-star will be hard, but not half as hard as getting through lunch without strangling the woman across the table from me. "He would make a good husband."

"Oh, you can tell that from across the room?" I ask, wondering how it is she can forget that when we had trouble getting rid of my last husband, she shot him. "Besides being ten minutes away from death if he actually eats all that steak, he's twenty years too old for me and—shallow woman that I am—twenty pounds too heavy. Besides, I am *so* not looking for another husband here. I'm looking to design a new image for this place, looking for some sense of ambience, some feeling, something I can build a proposal on for them."

My mother studies the man in the corner, tilting her head, the better to gauge his age, I suppose. I think she's grimacing, but with all the Botox and Restylane injected into that face, it's hard to tell. She takes another bite of her steak salad, chews slowly so that I don't miss the fact that the steak is a poor cut and tougher than it should be. "You're concentrating on the wrong kind of proposal," she says finally. "Just look at this place, Teddi. It's a dive. There are hardly any other diners. What does *that* tell you about the food?"

"That they cater to a dinner crowd and it's lunchtime," I tell her.

I don't know what I was thinking bringing her here with me. I suppose I thought it would be better than eating alone. There really are days when my common sense goes on vacation. Clearly, this is one of them. I mean, really, did I not resolve less than three weeks ago that I would not let my mother get to me anymore?

What good are New Year's resolutions, anyway?

Mario approaches the man's table and my mother studies him while they converse. Eventually Mario leaves the table with a huff, after which the diner glances up and meets my mother's gaze. I think she's smiling at him. That or she's got indigestion. They size each other up.

I concentrate on making sketches in my notebook and try to ignore the fact that my mother is flirting. At nearly seventy, she's developed an unhealthy interest in members of the opposite sex to whom she isn't married.

According to my father, who has broken the TMI rule and given me Too Much Information, she has no interest in sex with him. Better, I suppose, to be clued in on what they aren't doing in the bedroom than have to hear what they might be doing.

"He's not so old," my mother says, noticing that

I have barely touched the Chinese chicken salad she warned me not to get. "He's got about as many years on you as you have on your little cop friend."

She does this to make me crazy. I know it, but it works all the same. "Drew Scoones is not my little 'friend.' He's a detective with whom I—"

"Screwed around," my mother says. I must look shocked, because my mother laughs at me and asks if I think she doesn't know the "lingo."

What I thought she didn't know was that Drew and I actually tangled in the sheets. And, since it's possible she's just fishing, I sidestep the issue and tell her that Drew is just a couple of years younger than me and that I don't need reminding. I dig into my salad with renewed vigor, determined to show my mother that Chinese chicken salad in a steak place was not the stupid choice it's proving to be.

After a few more minutes of my picking at the wilted leaves on my plate, the man my mother has me nearly engaged to pays his bill and heads past us toward the back of the restaurant. I watch my mother take in his shoes, his suit and the diamond pinkie ring that seems to be cutting off the circulation in his little finger.

"Such nice hands," she says after the man is out of sight. "Manicured." She and I both stare at my hands. I have two popped acrylics that are being held on at weird angles by bandages. My cuticles are ragged and there's marker decorating my right hand from measuring carelessly when I did a drawing for a customer.

Twenty minutes later she's disappointed that he managed to leave the restaurant without our noticing. He will join the list of the ones I let get away. I will hear about him twenty years from now when—according to my mother—my children will be grown and I will still be single, living pathetically alone with several dogs and cats.

After my ex, that sounds good to me.

The waitress tells us that our meal has been taken care of by the management and, after thanking Mario, the owner, complimenting him on the wonderful meal and assuring him that once I have redecorated his place people will be flocking here in droves (I actually use those words and ignore my mother when she rolls her eyes), my mother and I head for the restroom.

My father—unfortunately not with us today— has the patience of a saint. He got it over the years of living with my mother. She, perhaps as a result, figures he has the patience for both of them, and feels justified having none. For her, no rules apply, and a little thing like a picture of a man on the door to a public restroom is certainly no barrier to using the john. In all fairness, it does seem silly to stand and wait for the ladies' room if no one is using the men's room.

Still, it's the idea that rules don't apply to her, signs don't apply to her, conventions don't apply to her. She knocks on the door to the men's room. When no one answers she gestures to me to go in ahead. I tell her that I can certainly wait for the ladies' room to be free and she shrugs and goes in herself.

Not a minute later there is a bloodcurdling scream from behind the men's room door.

"Mom!" I yell. "Are you all right?"

Mario comes running over, the waitress on his heels. Two customers head our way while my mother continues to scream.

I try the door, but it is locked. I yell for her to open it and she fumbles with the knob. When she finally manages to unlock and open it, she is white behind her two streaks of blush, but she is on her feet and appears shaken but not stirred.

"What happened?" I ask her. So do Mario and the waitress and the few customers who have migrated to the back of the place.

She points toward the bathroom and I go in, thinking it serves her right for using the men's room. But I see nothing amiss.

She gestures toward the stall, and, like any self-respecting and suspicious woman, I poke the door open with one finger, expecting the worst.

What I find is worse than the worst.

The husband my mother picked out for me is sitting on the toilet. His pants are puddled around his ankles, his hands are hanging at his sides. Pinned to his chest is some sort of Health Department certificate.

Oh, and there is a large, round, bloodless bullet hole between his eyes.

Four Nassau County police officers are securing the area, waiting for the detectives and crime scene personnel to show up. They are trying, though not very hard, to comfort my mother, who in another era would be considered to be suffering from the vapors. Less tactful in the twenty-first century, I'd say she was losing it. That is, if I didn't know her better, know she was milking it for everything it was worth.

My mother loves attention. As it begins to flag, she swoons and claims to feel faint. Despite four No Smoking signs, my mother insists it's all right for her to light up because, after all, she's in shock. Not to mention that signs, as we know, don't apply to her.

When asked not to smoke, she collapses mournfully in a chair and lets her head loll to the side, all without mussing her hair.

Eventually, the detectives show up to find the four patrolmen all circled around her, debating whether to administer CPR, smelling salts or simply call the paramedics. I, however, know just what will snap her to attention.

"Detective Scoones," I say loudly. My mother parts the sea of cops.

"We have to stop meeting like this," he says lightly to me, but I can feel him checking me over with his eyes, making sure I'm all right while pretending not to care.

"What have you got in those pants?" my mother asks him, coming to her feet and staring at his crotch accusingly. "*Baydar?* Everywhere we Bayers are, you turn up. You don't expect me to buy that this is a coincidence, I hope."

Drew tells my mother that it's nice to see her, too, and asks if it's his fault that her daughter seems to attract disasters.

Charming to be made to feel like the bearer of a plague.

He asks how I am.

"Just peachy," I tell him. "I seem to be making a habit of finding dead bodies, my mother is driving me crazy and the catering hall I booked two freakin' years ago for Dana's bat mitzvah has just been shut down by the Board of Health!"

"Glad to see your luck's finally changing," he says, giving me a quick squeeze around the shoulders before turning his attention to the patrolmen, asking what they've got, whether they've taken any statements, moved anything, all the sort of stuff you see on TV, without any of the drama. That is, if you don't count my mother's threats to faint every few minutes when she senses no one's paying attention to her.

Mario tells his waitstaff to bring everyone espresso, which I decline because I'm wired enough. Drew pulls him aside and a minute later I'm handed a cup of coffee that smells divinely of Kahlúa.

The man knows me well. Too well.

His partner, whom I've met once or twice, says he'll interview the kitchen staff. Drew asks Mario if he minds if he takes statements from the patrons first and gets to him and the waitstaff afterward.

"No, no," Mario tells him. "Do the patrons first."

Drew raises his eyebrow at me like he wants to know if I get the double entendre. I try to look bored.

"What is it with you and murder victims?" he asks me when we sit down at a table in the corner.

I search them out so that I can see you again, I almost say, but I'm afraid it will sound desperate instead of sarcastic.

My mother, lighting up and daring him with a look to tell her not to, reminds him that *she* was the one to find the body.

Drew asks what happened *this time.* My mother tells him how the man in the john was "taken" with me, couldn't take his eyes off me and blatantly flirted with both of us. To his credit, Drew doesn't laugh, but his smirk is undeniable to the trained eye. And I've had my eye trained on him for nearly a year now.

"While he was noticing you," he asks me, "did *you* notice anything about him? Was he waiting for anyone? Watching for anything?"

I tell him that he didn't appear to be waiting or watching. That he made no phone calls, was fairly intent on eating and did, indeed, flirt with my mother. This last bit Drew takes with a grain of salt, which was the way it was intended.

"And he had a short conversation with Mario,"

I tell him. "I think he might have been unhappy with the food, though he didn't send it back."

Drew asks what makes me think he was dissatisfied, and I tell him that the discussion seemed acrimonious and that Mario looked distressed when he left the table. Drew makes a note and says he'll look into it and asks about anyone else in the restaurant. Did I see anyone who didn't seem to belong, anyone who was watching the victim, anyone looking suspicious?

"Besides my mother?" I ask him, and Mom huffs and blows her cigarette smoke in my direction.

I tell him that there were several deliveries, the kitchen staff going in and out the back door to grab a smoke. He stops me and asks what I was doing checking out the back door of the restaurant.

Proudly—because, while he was off forgetting me, dropping by only once in a while to say hi to Jesse, my son, or drop something by for one of my daughters that he thought they might like, I was getting on with my life—I tell him that I'm decorating the place.

He looks genuinely impressed. "Commercial customers? That's great," he says. Okay, that's what he *ought* to say. What he actually says is "Whatever pays the bills."

"Howard Rosen, the famous restaurant critic, got her the job," my mother says. "You met him—the good-looking, distinguished gentleman with the *real* job, something to be proud of. I guess you've never read his reviews in *Newsday*."

Drew, without missing a beat, tells her that Howard's reviews are on the top of his list, as soon as he learns how to read.

"I only meant—" my mother starts, but both of us assure her that we know just what she meant.

"So," Drew says. "Deliveries?"

I tell him that Mario would know better than I, but that I saw vegetables come in, maybe fish and linens.

"This is the second restaurant job Howard's got her," my mother tells Drew.

"At least she's getting *something* out of the relationship," he says.

"If he were here," my mother says, ignoring the insinuation, "he'd be comforting her instead of interrogating her. He'd be making sure we're both all right after such an ordeal."

"I'm sure he would," Drew agrees, then looks me in the eyes as if he's measuring my tolerance for shock. Quietly he adds, "But then maybe he doesn't know just what strong stuff your daughter's made of."

It's the closest thing to a tender moment I can expect from Drew Scoones. My mother breaks the spell. "She gets that from me," she says.

Both Drew and I take a minute, probably to pray that's all I inherited from her.

"I'm just trying to save you some time and effort," my mother tells him. "My money's on Howard."

Drew withers her with a look and mutters something that sounds suspiciously like "fool's gold." Then he excuses himself to go back to work.

I catch his sleeve and ask if it's all right for us to leave. He says sure, he knows where we live. I say goodbye to Mario. I assure him that I will have some sketches for him in a few days, all the while hoping that this murder doesn't cancel his redecorating plans. I need the money desperately, the alternative being borrowing from my parents and being strangled by the strings.

My mother is strangely quiet all the way to her house. She doesn't tell me what a loser Drew Scoones is—despite his good looks—and how I was obviously drooling over him. She doesn't ask me where Howard is taking me tonight or warn me not to tell my father about what happened because he will worry about us both and no doubt insist we see our respective psychiatrists.

She fidgets nervously, opening and closing her purse over and over again.

"You okay?" I ask her. After all, she's just found a dead man on the toilet, and tough as she is that's got to be upsetting.

When she doesn't answer me I pull over to the side of the road.

"Mom?" She refuses to meet my eyes. "You want me to take you to see Dr. Cohen?"

She looks out the window as if she's just realized we're on Broadway in Woodmere. "Aren't we near Marvin's Jewelers?" she asks, pulling something out of her purse.

"What have you got, Mother?" I ask, prying open her fingers to find the murdered man's ring.

"It was on the sink," she says in answer to my dropped jaw. "I was going to get his name and address and have you return it to him so that he could ask you out. I thought it was a sign that the two of you were meant to be together."

"He's dead, Mom. You understand that, right?" I ask. You never can tell when my mother is fine and when she's in la-la land.

"Well, I didn't know that," she shouts at me. "Not at the time."

I ask why she didn't give it to Drew, realize that she wouldn't give Drew the time in a clock shop and add, "...or one of the other policemen?"

"For heaven's sake," she tells me. "The man is dead, Teddi, and I took his ring. How would that look?"

Before I can tell her it looks just the way it is, she pulls out a cigarette and threatens to light it.

"I mean, really," she says, shaking her head like it's my brains that are loose. "What does he need with it now?"

Silhouette®

SPECIAL EDITION™

Logan's Legacy Revisited

**THE LOGAN FAMILY IS BACK
WITH SIX NEW STORIES.**

Beginning in January 2007 with

THE COUPLE MOST LIKELY TO

by

LILIAN DARCY

Tragedy drove them apart. Reunited eighteen
years later, their attraction was once again
undeniable. But had time away changed
Jake Logan enough to let him face his fears
and commit to the woman he once loved?

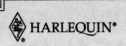

Happily Ever After
Is Just the Beginning…

Harlequin Books brings you stories of love
that stand the test of time. Find books by
some of your favorite series authors and
by exciting new authors who'll soon
become favorites, too. Each story spans years
and will take you on an emotional journey
that starts with falling in love.

If you're a romantic at heart, you'll
definitely want to read this new series!

Every great love has a story to tell.™

Two new titles every month
LAUNCHING FEBRUARY 2007

Available wherever series books are sold.

nocturne™

**WAS HE HER SAVIOR
OR HER NIGHTMARE?**

HAUNTED
LISA CHILDS

Years ago, Ariel and her sisters were separated for
their own protection. Now the man who vowed
revenge on her family has resumed the hunt, and
Ariel must warn her sisters before it's too late.
The closer she comes to finding them, the more
secretive her fiancé becomes. Can she trust the man
she plans to spend eternity with? Or has he been
waiting for the perfect moment to destroy her?

On sale December 2006.